HECK
SUPERHERO

MARTINE LEAVITT

BOYDS MILLS PRESS
AN IMPRINT OF HIGHLIGHTS
Honesdale, Pennsylvania

I am indebted to *Wizard: the Comic Magazine,* which enlarged
my understanding of the multiverse of comic art. Heck and I
would also like to thank Stephen Roxburgh and all the secret
superheroes at Vermont College.

Copyright © 2004 by Martine Leavitt
Cover illustrations copyright © by iStock.com
All rights reserved
For information about permission to reproduce selections from this book,
please contact permissions@highlights.com.
Printed in the United States of America
Designed by Helen Robinson
First paperback edition, 2014

Library of Congress Cataloging-in-Publication Data
Leavitt, Martine
Heck superhero / by Martine Leavitt.
p. cm.
Summary: Abandoned by his mother, thirteen-year-old Heck
tries to survive on his own as his mind bounces between the superhero
character he imagines himself to be and the harsh reality of his life.
ISBN-13: 978-1-886910-94-2 (hc) • 978-1-62979-109-8 (pb)
[1. Abandoned children–Fiction. 2. Cartoons and comics–Fiction.
3. Emotional problems–Fiction. 4. Art–Fiction. 5. Canada–Fiction.] I. Title.

PZ7. L4656He 2003
[Fic]-dc21   2002192863

Boyds Mills Press, Inc.
An Imprint of Highlights
815 Church Street
Honesdale, Pennsylvania 18431

10 9 8 7 6 5 4 3 2 1

This book is dedicated to the super seventh,
Dallas Dean

"The loved one herself becomes for him a melody, a fixed idea which keeps coming back to him and which he hears everywhere."
—from the program notes for Hector Berlioz's *Fantastic Symphony*

Monday, May 2

Question: How do you rescue a mom from hypertime?
Answer: You have to be a superhero.

Heck wasn't a superhero, or if he was, he was definitely in his flat stage, his no-curves-no-life-dead-on-the-page stage. Of course, all superheroes started out that way. It said so in his *How to Draw Superheroes* book. Before the costume and the muscles, before the piping and the overlines, there was a stick man, flat on the page, lifeless. Right now, Heck felt like a stick man, so flat he wondered how he managed not to slip through the slats of the mall bench he was sitting on. A toothache could do that to you. A toothache, and missing breakfast and lunch, and not knowing where your mom stayed last night.

He remembered where the Pepper Bar was, where his mom worked. As soon as it was time for school to be out, he'd go there. He'd talk to her. "Don't worry, Mom," he'd say, "everything's okay. Everything's going to be okay."

Heck pulled out the twenty-dollar bill and smoothed it over his knee. He had been almost surprised this morning, waking up in Mr. Hill's car, to find it still in his pocket.

Stolen. From his best friend, Spence. You couldn't get any flatter than that. He'd never stolen anything before. You couldn't be a thief and a superhero at the same time.

Why had he taken it? It must have been his mom's voice when she called him at Spence's yesterday. "They've locked us out, Heck. Ask if you can stay there for a day or two, will you, while I get some things straightened out?" she'd said.

Heck hadn't said anything. Not "No." Not "You ask them." Not "Okay, sure." Just nothing. Everything he wanted to say was in a word bubble over his head, but she couldn't read bubble over the phone.

"Thanks, Heck," she'd said to his silence. "Thanks, baby. I'll call you soon, okay? You're my hero." She hung up.

"What?" Spence had asked, looking hard at him.

"Nothing ..." They'd received envelopes from Mr. Grenhold, the landlord, but his mom just put them in a bill pile and ignored them. Heck knew it was notices. He just didn't want to know.

Spence's mom had stopped peeling potatoes—she was always peeling something—and looked sharply at Heck. The bubble over his head popped and he felt letters fall on him like rain.

"Nothing," Heck had repeated.

"Okay, let's get back to the game," Spence had said.

"What is it, Heck?" Mrs. Carter had asked.

Here we go, he'd thought.

"You know you can always talk to us."

Heck's mom wanted him to stay there, but she wouldn't

want them to know her business.

"Everything's okay," Heck had said, even though he had this heavy feeling in his stomach like his heart just fell into it and his left ventricle was being slowly digested.

Mrs. Carter had looked at him a long moment. Heck had pasted a smile on his face and she'd started peeling again.

He and Spence had gone back to playing video games, but Heck didn't do very well.

"Guess I'm finally getting better than you," Spence said gleefully. "You're not letting me win, are you? This isn't one of your crazy Good Deeds or something, is it? Because if it is ..."

"No," Heck said. As casually as he could he said, "Do you think your parents would let me sleep over again tonight?"

"No, my parents consider Sunday a school night," Spence said. With a tap of the button his video-game character dealt the final blow. Spence cheered. "Yes! For once I'm going to beat you!"

That night Spence's dad had dropped Heck off in front of the apartment as usual. For just a moment, before he got out of the car, Heck thought of telling, but he couldn't. What if it wasn't only a couple of days? His mom had this thing with time—she and it didn't get along.

He had recognized that tone in her voice, the one that said, "I'm in hypertime and I don't know when I'll be back." Her friend Dierdre called it depression.

But Heck had learned by reading comics that hypertime was a bridge to coexisting realities. It was how Superman could be dead in one comic book issue and alive in the next. Both were true, each in its own time and existence. It meant he could have a mom who was the best mom a kid could dream up and the kind of mom that Social Services had a file on. When he'd heard her voice last night, he knew. She was feeling like she couldn't deal with this microverse full of evil landlords who changed locks and evicted her from her apartment.

Last time she went into hypertime was when he got sent home with a note from the teacher saying he didn't have a proper coat and would she please do something about it. His mom went into the living room, sat on the couch, turned on the TV, and didn't do anything for a week. It was all Heck could do to get her to drink tea and eat crackers and cheese.

Heck Superhero, lost and abandoned in the world of mortals, without his supersuit and the tokens of his strength ...

Heck sat up straight and looked around the mall. No one was looking at him, but he could almost hear Mr. Bandras's voice: "Daydreaming again, Heck? There's a time and a place for that, and this isn't it."

Heck had to admit that now was not a good time to be daydreaming. Not when they'd lost their apartment and when his portfolio with all his semester artwork was locked in it and when bacteria were mining their way down through his molars and into his jawbone. He had to stay in this microverse and take care of his mom. Flat or not, he had to get to his mom soon. He had to get her out of hypertime, keep her from thinking crazy stuff like that he was better off without her or something. He had to talk to her before she floated like a dry leaf right out of this dimension.

He had to think, make a plan, a good plan, a smart plan—a superplan ...

There was always the Good Deed.

Of course, there was that bad deed still in his pocket to worry about.

A delicious smell from the mall's food court drifted right up his nostrils. He was hungry.

He'd been hungry before, but not this hungry. He felt turned inside out, like his stomach was on the outside of him and his human face on the inside. Being this hungry put his stomach in charge of his brain and his hands and his feet. If you weren't a superhero, being this hungry could make you spend the money you stole from your best friend ...

Heck felt the twenty in his pocket. He looked around. None of the people walking by seemed to be able to tell that he was harboring stolen goods. He thought about phoning Spence. He'd say, "Hey, guess what I accidentally found in my pocket? Are you missing a twenty? Isn't that strange? How could that have happened? I'll be right over." Would that be a Good Deed? No, it would just be canceling out a bad deed, putting it in the category of "doing the right thing after having done the wrong thing."

An announcement came over the mall intercom: "There is a lost child, wearing a navy wool coat and black shoes ..." Heck wondered if there was a citywide intercom that could announce, "Attention, flat superhero looking for small apartment that requires no references ..."

He was about to take out the twenty again when a woman

walked by. She was old and white-haired, just the sort of lady you'd want to do a Good Deed for if you were a superhero. He smiled and said, "Good afternoon."

She smiled back and threw something in the trash can near him. Something that hit the trash with a soft, sandwichy heaviness.

Heck waited until she was far enough away, and then he looked in.

Egg salad. A whole half, not even bitten into. Heck pulled it out and bit in.

Egg salad. Surely the egg salad sandwich was the most delicious food ever invented by man. It was a marvel, a wonder, the egg salad sandwich, and no technological advance could match this pinnacle of achievement. Heck's brain genuflected before the genius of whoever invented bread. Strange that they had never learned that in Social Studies. There should be at least one class devoted to the mastermind who invented bread. What about the person who first whipped up a batch of mayonnaise? Why wasn't there a statue of her somewhere?

The Good Deed. It was still working for him. A simple smile and a good afternoon to a little old lady, and—egg salad! But now that he had a little egg salad in his system, one thing was clear: no Good Deed was good enough to help him find his mom until he'd fixed the bad one. He had to give back the twenty and confess to Spence.

His skin was goose-bumpy with pleasure as he ate the last bite.

Now he could think.

Spence would be home from school by now, and wondering why Heck hadn't been there today.

He couldn't go to school. He didn't have his books. They were locked up in the apartment. He didn't have paper or a pen or a lunch or a shower or deodorant or a toothbrush, essential items for school attendance. Especially he didn't have his artist's portfolio with his semester artwork in it, which had to be turned in on Friday. He could imagine the look on Mr. Bandras's face when he told him his dog ate ten pounds' worth of paper and paint.

Mr. Bandras would know. "You don't have a dog," he would say. He would see. He would ask. It was better to let the school think he was under quarantine for scarlet fever or something. Besides, it wasn't bad having a day off school, especially when they didn't even teach you about the invention of the egg salad sandwich. He bet Mrs. Bandras could make a mean egg salad sandwich.

He pulled the change out of his pocket. His mom always made sure he had enough to call her from a pay phone—in an emergency, she said. He walked around the phone a few times. Even though they were molecularly joined, it was hard sometimes to predict what Spence would do. Heck still remembered the day he and Spence became molecularly joined through a super mind meld. Spence didn't call it that. He said, "It's freaky how we get each other."

Heck picked up the receiver and hung it up again.

The egg salad had settled into the holes of his back teeth and was bubbling itself into frothing, burning acid. He was sure if he had superhearing he'd be able to hear the enamel fizzing as it was being eaten away. He had to keep his mouth closed. The conditioned air of the mall felt as cold as ice water on his teeth. The exposed roots began to squeal in little high-pitched voices, louder even than the mall music.

He punched his jaw. He should have known better than to eat.

He picked up the receiver again.

He dialed the number.

"Hello?"

"It's me."

"Where were you today?" Spence asked. Heck never missed school. Being sick put too much stress on his mom.

"Sick," Heck said.

"You've been that way for years."

Hearing his voice was almost as good as egg salad. "Did you know that you have an egg salad kind of voice?" Heck asked.

"What?" Spence laughed. A good sign. "So what are you sick with?"

"Uh ... chicken pox," Heck said.

"Chicken pox? Doesn't that keep you from ever having children or something?"

"No, you can have children, but they'll peck at their food."

"Funny," Spence said. "What's up, Heck?" Spence wasn't buying the sick thing. He was too sharp for that. "Is something going on?"

No. Nothing. Except that my mom and I have been evicted

and I don't know where she's staying or who's taking care of her ... "It's okay. You don't have to worry," Heck said.

"I'm not worried." Spence said, but his voice was suddenly wary.

"Don't worry later."

"Okay, that's it. What's going on?"

He should tell. Heck knew he should. But if he told and his mom didn't call, didn't come to get him, she might get in trouble. When she was in hypertime, she couldn't keep track of real time. What if a couple of days stretched into three, or four, or ten? Would Spence's parents call Social Services? The police? His mom would be arrested or something and he'd end up in a frosty home. That was what he'd called the foster home as a little kid when his mom had gone into hypertime and left him at an emergency daycare for three weeks.

"Hey, Spence, does your mom ever make you egg salad sandwiches for lunch?"

"Huh? No. I don't like egg salad."

"See, that is the sort of thing that makes me worry about you, Spence."

"You are making no sense today," Spence said. "What's with you?"

"Spence, I need to ask you a hypothetical question. If a friend stole money from you, would you ever be able to forgive him?"

"You stole money from me?"

"Listen, I—I've got to go, Spence. I'll call you later." He hung up.

—

Heck's teeth sang every note of the mall's pumped-in music, only on a scale so high the notes felt like needles. His left ear was beginning to ache.

Heck punched his jaw. Flatter than ever. What kind of superhero couldn't own up to his misdeeds?

It was almost time to go find his mom at the Pepper Bar. They'd get everything straightened out, and in three months Heck would tell Spence all about it in a way that would make him laugh and this whole thing would be over.

He punched his jaw again. While he was in the Pepper Bar he'd ask Levi on the sly for an aspirin. He didn't want to worry his mom about his teeth. That would be the last straw.

He'd eat, too. He had to feed his mortal alter ego. For sure, being hungry could turn the roundest brain into lasagna noodles.

Lasagna ...

Almost without thinking about it, Heck stood up and walked to a trash can. He pulled out a pizza box when he thought no one was looking. There were crusts still in it, and some pineapple stuck to the box. Heck sat down with it on the bench.

"That's dirty," someone said.

Heck turned to see a little girl staring at him. She was wearing a navy coat and shiny black shoes.

"It's dirty to eat things out of the garbage," she said.

Not dirty, Heck thought. Flat. "I wasn't going to eat it," he said. "I was ... I was just going to use the box to draw on." He pulled out his sketching pencil. "See?"

The little girl looked him in the eye, opened her mouth, and wailed. Her face didn't scrunch up, and there were no tears in her eyes.

"What?" Heck asked.

She stopped wailing. "I'm lost," she said. She started to wail again, scrunchless and tearless. Shoppers passed by without noticing.

"Hey. Hey, don't cry. Here, I'll draw you, okay?"

She stopped. Heck took a good look. She had black eyes a color you couldn't buy and brown skin a color you couldn't mix. Heck began to sketch, and after a minute he felt her at his side.

She pointed. "Is that me?"

"Yes," Heck said. "You are the Good Deed."

The girl watched in silence a little longer. "Who's that?"

He smiled. "That's me, Heck Superhero."

She looked at the picture and then at him and back at the picture again. "It doesn't look like you."

"I'm in my flat stage right now," Heck said.

"What are you doing?"

"Saving you."

"Oh." In a moment she asked, "From what?"

"Evil forces."

"Oh," she said.

Heck sketched fast. It made his teeth feel better to draw. It made everything feel better to draw. "See, if I save you, then maybe the curse will be lifted and Heck Superhero will go live with his fellow heroes in the topworld."

The little girl sighed.

"What?" he asked.

"Evil forces have got inside my shoes."

"Your feet hurt?"

She nodded.

"I hate it when that happens," Heck said. He handed her the drawing. "What's your name?"

"Wanda."

"Wanda? Okay, Wanda Woman, let's go find your mom."

It wasn't long before he saw a security guard with a radio, and beside him a woman with brown skin a color you couldn't mix. She saw Heck and the girl before the guard did, and came running toward them. The little girl met her halfway, the pizza-box drawing still in her hand.

The security guard stared at Heck as he approached. Heck knew what he must be thinking: pervert or good-deed-doer? Maybe if he thought Heck was a sicko, they'd take him in for questioning like on TV and Heck would offer to confess everything in exchange for tacos and a gallon of milk.

"Where did you find her?" the woman asked as she drew her daughter into her arms.

"Just over there, ma'am," Heck said, gesturing. Superheroes always said ma'am and sir. It was part of their job description.

"Look, Momma! See what he drew for me? That's me, Wanda Woman."

"Thank you," the woman said to Heck. "Thank you very

much." The little girl chattered on about evil forces.

The security guard looked Heck over, consulted his watch. "Don't you have school this time of day?" he asked.

"Professional development day," Heck said.

To her daughter the woman said, "Yes, he is a hero to us, isn't he, sweetheart." She glanced up at Heck. "Thank you again."

"Bye, Superhero!" the little girl called as they walked away.

The security guard said something into his radio, then hooked it onto his belt. He put a heavy hand on Heck's shoulder. "Done with your shopping?"

Heck searched the word bubble over his head. There was nothing in it but white space.

The guard thumped Heck's shoulder in a friendly but dismissive sort of way, and then made a long gesture for Heck to move along.

Heck left the mall and headed to the Pepper Bar.

Helping the little girl get back to her mom was a Good Deed. It wasn't *the* Good Deed, the one that would get him and his mom topworld, but something good would come to him for it. Now if only he didn't still have that twenty in his pocket reminding him of past dastardly deeds.

He hadn't meant to take it. The Carters kept a little money in the drawer of a small table in the entranceway. He'd known that for a long time, since the first time he was invited to Spence's house. If Spence needed change for things, he knew to find it there. Sometimes there were a few quarters, and sometimes there were bills. Heck had always loved that they had money to just leave around, money that had no particular use, money they could just sort of forget was there. On his way out the door last night, Heck opened the drawer, just to look at it. Jackpot. Three twenties, a ten, and a million pennies and nickels. Then he heard Spence coming, and he'd just stuffed a twenty in his pocket. Aargh.

Heck hoped the restaurant wasn't too busy yet. He'd need a good ten, fifteen minutes to pull her out of hypertime, make her laugh, tell her about getting a good grade on a test, tell her he was sure glad they were out of that dumpy apartment. He'd tell her how happy Spence was to have weekday sleepovers, and he'd find out where she was staying.

He'd say everything's okay, like he always did.

He almost ran the last few blocks, and flung open the door to the Pepper Bar. Levi was leaning over the cash counter, and the place was practically empty. Oh, man, it smelled good.

"Hey, Heck, what brings you here?"

Levi was possibly the ugliest man on the planet, but he could cook hideously delicious things that made you want to kiss his ring in gratitude.

"I need to talk to my mom," Heck said. He was puffing from walking so long and fast.

"She's not here, Heck," Levi said.

"When does her shift start?"

He looked at Heck strangely. "It doesn't."

"She doesn't work today? But ..."

"She came in yesterday and said she needed a vacation. I told her she'd already taken all her vacation time for the year. She said she'd give up next year's ... You know, Heck, I like your mom, but I've got to have people I can rely on. I told her if she didn't come in this morning, she was out of a job."

A vacation.

Levi continued. "She's a good waitress, the best, it's just I get a knot in my stomach every day wondering if she's going to be here or not. This vacation thing was the last straw." He seemed apologetic, sad even, but Heck felt too flat to tell him he understood.

"Did she say anything else?" Heck asked in flat.

Levi shook his head. "She didn't say much at all. She seemed real sad about something. I asked her if she felt okay, but she just left." He was peering at Heck as if he'd just discovered a new life form. "You hungry? I've got some stuffed peppers just out of the oven."

Maybe his Little Girl Good Deed had added up to this: one stuffed pepper. He nodded.

Levi disappeared into the kitchen.

His mom was in hypertime. No doubt about it now. It always started out that way—she'd get sad, couldn't go to work, couldn't shower.

He had to find her fast, before she got too tempted by that other dimension in which she didn't exist. When she saw him, she'd know she loved him too much to get all the way there.

Where would she go?

Levi returned carrying a plate with the biggest pepper Heck had ever seen. Bursting out of the top of it was a mixture of rice and beef and onions and mushrooms. Heck hated beef, but he had never smelled anything so tempting in his life. He thought he might faint at the smell of it. It was kryptonite to him—now he could hardly lift his fork.

"Eat up," Levi said. "It's on the house."

Heck cut into the pepper. Every organ of his body was shivering with anticipation, except his stomach. It was like he'd swallowed the word "vacation" and it was taking up all the room in his belly.

He swallowed one little bite. His toes were screaming, "Food! Food!" in corny high voices. His kneecaps were spasming with pleasure, and his little taste buds were blossoming. His stomach, though, didn't seem to have room for much more than that one bite.

He swallowed another bite anyway. It went down, but his stomach didn't like it.

Levi went in and out of the kitchen. After a while he came and sat next to Heck. "Isn't it good?"

Heck nodded. "It's great. Really great."

Levi rubbed his whiskers. "Are you feeling all right, Heck?"

"Fine. Fine." Swallow.

"Do you need some money?"

Heck stopped, mid-chew.

Trap. Do-gooder trap: "Let me help you in exchange for

information that will then get you into trouble." Heck could hear a trap a mile away. Don't tell, he told himself. It would make it worse on her if he told. Besides, he'd just figured it out. She was probably at Dierdre's. He should have gone there first.

He shook his head. "I'm okay." The rice was waking his teeth up. What if she wasn't at Dierdre's? Where else would she go? Who else did she know? "Levi, do you remember that guy Mom went out with a month ago? His name was Sam or something."

"Met him once."

"Where does he work?"

"Don't know. Guess she doesn't talk about these things with you?"

"Do you know where he lives?"

"I don't ... Wait a minute. Yeah, I know where he lives. Your mom asked me to mail her last paycheck there. Hold on." Levi went to the cash register and took a piece of paper from an envelope. "Here it is. Sam Halstead. Address of 356 Morrow Drive. I know that area a bit. It's over by the old Lindsay Park."

Heck took another bite and stood up. There was a hot spot developing on his left cheek. "Thanks, Levi."

"Aren't you going to finish?"

"I'm full. But thank you. It was great."

"You want some dessert?" Levi asked, but Heck was on his way out, the door already closing behind him.

—

Heck headed back to the mall. Why would she have her check mailed there? Sam wasn't a boyfriend—she'd just dated him a few times. Maybe she thought it would be safer to send it to Sam's than to Dierdre's. Dierdre tended to lose things. Also, his mom knew Dierdre would be tipped off if the check came there. Dierdre would guess something was wrong.

He had to phone Dierdre's. For sure his mom would be there.

He didn't have a quarter for the phone.

What would he say to her anyway? Hey, Mom, heard you lost your job?

He had to have some good news. If he had a job, for instance, that would be good news. That was it—he'd get a job! Not just a flyer-delivery job like he'd been trying to get before. It had to be a real job.

Besides, if he had a job, he could spend the twenty and pay Spence back later.

All superheroes had a day job. They had to earn a living somehow in the guise of their alter egos.

He remembered that he'd seen a Help Wanted notice in the window of the Art Store, the warehouse-sized place where the high school art competition was being held. He'd get a job like that, get a place, take care of himself. He'd always been able to take care of himself pretty well anyway. He'd tell Spence he quit school on purpose to get this job, he'd invite Spence to a sleepover on a school night, and in the fridge would be peanut butter for Spence and a big bowl of egg salad for himself.

It seemed simple and obvious.

Heck slumped into the mall, found his bench, and then shrank down into his hoodie as the security guard walked by. The guard looked in his direction but didn't see him. Such a thing probably happened all the time to flat, two-dimensional beings living in a three-dimensional world: at just the right angle you became practically invisible.

Heck pulled the twenty out again. He hated to break it, but he really needed to phone Dierdre's, where for sure his mom would be.

"You're having a hard time figuring out what to do with that twenty, aren't you."

Heck stared. It was a girl, but not a little one this time. She had hair as short as a boy's, but he never saw anyone who looked so much like a girl. She was wearing pink sneakers. Just the sort of girl you'd like to do a Good Deed for.

"Pardon?"

"I can help you spend that," she said.

"It's not my money."

She sat on the bench close to him. He sat still as a life-sized poster.

She smiled. Her teeth were rounded at the tips, not straight and sharp like most people's. She was Girl at its roundest: round head, round eyes, round just right everywhere else.

"You skipping school today?"

"How did you know?"

"I saw you here earlier, when you should have been in school."

He cleared his throat. "I don't go to school," he said. "I'm getting a job in an art gallery." It sounded good to say it.

She nodded. "I see," she said, in a way that told him she didn't see at all. "That was a good picture you drew, of the little girl, the superhero. I walked by when you were drawing it."

Heck smiled a little and shrugged.

"Will you draw me?" she asked.

Heck felt himself blush all the way down to his armpits. People often asked him that, but he usually didn't draw where others could see. Drawing, for Heck, required more than looking. It was a kind of Good Deed because you had to see—really see—to draw someone.

"Nah."

"Please?" She put her hand on his knee.

He shook his head.

Her eyes narrowed. "You drew for that other girl."

"Superhero stuff," he said.

That was what he usually drew, even in art class. Mr. Bandras gave him near-perfect grades on everything he produced that wasn't a superhero. He'd have the top grade in the class if his semester artwork weren't locked up in his ex-apartment.

He punched his jaw.

"Why do you do that?" she asked.

"Toothache," he said.

"I've got something that can make you feel better," she said. She held out her hand and in the middle of it was one round green pill.

"They're called Supermans," she said. "Only costs twenty dollars."

Heck put his hand in his pocket and gripped his pencil. Velocity Nine. Sure enough, the pill had Superman's S symbol imprinted into it. "You got any aspirin?" he asked.

"This is better," she said.

Heck shook his head at the floor between his feet. There was no air in his flat throat. He tried to smile.

"You've never done anything before?" she asked incredulously.

"I've done stuff before," Heck said. No, he hadn't.

"This'll make your teeth feel better," she said. "It will make you feel good all over."

"I try not to do drugs on days that end in y," Heck said. He and Spence had read that in a comic book. Spence made Heck practice saying it. "That way it will come naturally for you," Spence had said.

"How old are you?"

"Thirteen."

The girl frowned. She closed her fist around the pill. "No wonder. You're just a little kid," she said.

"For all I know, you may be an undercover cop," Heck said. They'd practiced that one, too. Spence seemed to think Heck was gullible or something. His teeth throbbed.

"Twenty bucks isn't worth all this," she said. She stood up.

What if he just gave it to her? Was it a Good Deed if you gave away stolen money? Spence didn't believe in the Good Deed the way Heck did, but he was a nice guy. He'd probably give it to her.

"Hey, you can have the twenty if you really need it," he said.

Spence didn't mind the odd small Good Deed, so long as it didn't get out of hand. He'd pay Spence back later, after he got his first paycheck.

He held out the twenty to her. "Use it to start a new drug-free life," he said. "I just need a quarter out of that to use the phone."

Just then Heck saw the security guard walking in their direction, still a way off. The girl saw him too. She snatched the twenty.

"Thanks," she said. "See ya."

"Hey!" Heck called. "I really need that change." She just kept walking. He didn't want to chase after her—the security guard would notice him for sure.

He pulled his hood over his head and watched her walk away. He wasn't sure if he felt good because of the Good Deed or lousy because he just gave his friend's money away.

He decided he felt good. Somehow change for the phone would come to him for that Good Deed.

He closed his lips so the air wouldn't touch his teeth.

Maybe he could ask one of the mall shoppers, someone who looked like he had a quarter he could spare. All of them looked like they had places to go. None of them walked on the world like it was going to crack. None of them seemed to live under a curse that made them have to justify their share of the planet's oxygen ...

He saw the pill. She'd left it there, sitting in plain view on the bench beside him.

He sucked in a big gulp of mall air. Cold filled the holes in his teeth. He closed his mouth, but his teeth wouldn't stop screaming.

The security guard was close. Heck put the pill in his pocket just as he strode by.

Heck punched his jaw, but it didn't help.

He punched again, harder.

His jawbone trembled, his nasal passages vibrated, his teeth thrilled like flutes.

Heck folded his arms over his head. His tongue probed the holes in his teeth. Every bone in his head played the drums.

He took the escalator to the lower level of the mall. Behind the escalators there was a maze of medical offices. He walked the halls until he found a dentist. Dr. B. J. R. Murdock, D.D.S. There was a big smiling tooth painted on the window and a sign that said, "We Cater to Cowards."

He passed that one, and walked into the next dentist's office he came to.

He was sure the receptionist could hear his teeth, as if he had a personal CD player turned up too loud and the sound was leaking out of the headphones.

"Yes, can I help you?" she asked.

"I was going to ask you the same thing," he said. When your teeth hurt this bad, you didn't care what people thought about you. "Can I help you? Need any Good Deeds?"

"Good what?"

Heck swallowed. "Uh—any odd jobs need doing around

here? In exchange for dental work?"

She looked puzzled for a moment, then smiled and shook her head. "Um, no, I don't think so."

Maybe the dentist was the doer of Good Deeds for other people. "Do you fill teeth for people who don't have any money?" Heck asked.

She looked at him like he had a spider on his face. "No, I'm sorry, we don't, but I believe you can call Social Services in the blue pages—"

"You can't call," Heck said. He'd tried once before when he didn't want to worry his mom. Somehow, then, the pain went away, but now it had returned with a vengeance. "All you get is a hostile machine. It tells you to do all this stuff—send it income tax returns ... I don't have an income tax return."

"I'm sorry, I wish we could—"

"I went to Community Assistance," continued Heck, "but they don't fill. They only pull. If I go to Community Assistance they'll assist me until I don't have any teeth left."

She stared blankly at him.

"Do you give out pain medication?" Heck asked.

"Young man, I'm sorry, but ..."

She kept saying she was sorry, but she didn't seem very sorry. "Can you take me to your leader?"

She glared at him then, and he knew she was thinking that maybe he was carrying a flat handgun or a very thin rifle or ...

She picked up the phone and said something, and in a moment a big man came out to the desk. He had thick black hair on his arms and was wearing green surgical clothes.

"Is there a problem here?"

"I think alien forces have begun their scheme to supplant the human race by germ warfare, and they've started in my mouth," Heck said. "See?" He opened his mouth wide.

The dentist folded his arms. "So, now you know the real reason why we invented dental floss. All this stuff about plaque is just a coverup."

Heck didn't smile. "I could do odd jobs in exchange for dental work."

The dentist considered him a moment. "Look," he said, "we're not exactly set up to help you here. But if you bring your mom in, maybe we can work something out."

"She's—she's pretty busy. Could you just give me something, maybe? For the pain?"

"Bring your mom in, and we'll see what we can do to help," he said. His voice sounded like a teacher's when the discussion was supposed to be over.

Heck stood there a moment. "Okay. Thanks," he said. As he walked out he thought he heard the dentist say, "Harmless enough."

Heck leaned against a wall.

Bring your mom in. An easy enough task if you lived in a microverse without time loops. Impossible, though, if you had a mom who counted at a right angle to real numbers and lived in imaginary time.

He felt in his pocket for the pill.

He wasn't going to swallow it. He just wanted to look at it.

He felt for it, but it wasn't there, and he was glad, but then it was. He pulled it out, all coated with blue pocket lint.

Found.

Round.

It weighed a pound.

That was a poem. It rolled around.

Maybe he should take the pill. Maybe he wouldn't get too high because the pain would hold him down like a stone on the string of a helium balloon. Besides, why shouldn't he take the pill? He'd paid for it. Not willingly, maybe, but Spence's money was gone.

No.

Bad for him. Bad, bad, bad.

But ... who cared?

Yeah, and besides that, who cared?

Furthermore, who cared?

Who cared about a flat-broke bottomworld garbage-eater? His mom? She was probably just now noticing that she hadn't seen him for a while. So, one might ask, who cared? Heck? Heck, no.

Heck swallowed the pill.

Right away he wished he hadn't done it.

Right away he knew what Spence would say to him. He'd say, Hello, billiard ball brain. He'd say, How are you, Hi-Ho Lord Emperor of Stupid? He'd say, Do you like your brains fried or scrambled?

And what about his mom? How would he take care of his

mom if he was starting a life of crime and addiction?

He walked to his bench. He'd stay here and not move until it was all over. No matter what happened, he'd stay where he was.

Half an hour later, everything was still the same except that he didn't feel hungry anymore and his teeth weren't as noisy. He was relieved. The round girl had probably just given him a birth control pill or something and at that very moment he was chemically mutating and all his future children would be born with golf-ball-sized heads.

Everything was okay. He just needed to find a quarter so he could phone Dierdre. Come and get me, Dierdre, he'd say. I need to talk to my mom. He didn't feel tired anymore. He felt ... "Compassionate," he said aloud.

Yes, compassion was what he felt as he watched the mortal shoppers who shuffled by on feet that could not fly and saw through eyes that could not pierce brick.

He would do a Good Deed for one of them. Yes. He would.

Just thinking about the Good Deed made him feel better. It was the cookie at the bottom of the bag. It was the holiday coming up, the good dream the night before, the money in the pocket of a coat you hadn't worn for a long time. It was the thing that made you feel good even though you couldn't remember what it was that was making you feel good. It was a big stupid smile in his brain and he couldn't help it. It came down to this: if you did a true Good Deed, you could change the microverse, maybe change it to a better one.

It could cure crime. Take a wrongdoer, put him in a pink cell, and just do Good Deeds to him all day long until his evil dried up. All the out-of-work grandmothers could do it. They could knit him sweaters and feed him chicken and dumplings and apple pie and read him stories until he was brought to his knees. Evil could never thrive under intensive Good Deed Therapy.

Not long ago, Heck had figured out a way that it could cure the common cold. Everyone thought about ways to *fight* germs, but what if they invented a sort of germ cookie, something that germs liked eating even more than they liked human cells? You could entice them to eat the germ cookies, and give them their own country in Antarctica. Same with cancer—feed the cancer something tasty so it didn't have to dine on human nuclei.

Yes, the Good Deed was the Theory of Everything, and he was just the superhero to get the job done.

Heck fixed his eye on the clerk in the men's wear store across from his bench. All the time he'd been sitting there, not one person had gone into her store. There she stood, nothing to do, no one to talk to. Poor mortal thing.

He walked into the store.

"May I help you?" the clerk asked brightly. Her name tag said Jennifer.

"I am the one who helps," Heck said. It sounded so true. She seemed not to understand him, and then she smiled as if it didn't matter.

"All our shirts are half price today," she said, "and then there's our Super Discount rack."

"Yes. Super. That's what I need," Heck said. He followed her, but suddenly he knew nothing in this store would fit him. He was rounding out big time.

"This would look good on you," Jennifer said, pulling out a black shirt.

"Black's taken. Batman already has black," Heck said.

"Excuse me?"

"The Lantern has green, Spiderman has red, Superman has blue ..."

She stared at him a moment and then quietly put the shirt back on the rack. She shuffled through the rack as if looking for a color that hadn't been taken.

"I'm not sure we have anything for you," she said in a small voice.

"Maybe I should go to Mr. Big and Tall," Heck said.

"Yes," she said, concentrating on a price tag, "that's a good idea."

Something in her voice made him think about what he was saying. Why had he even come in here? He should be looking for his mom. What about his plan to find a job? Here he was doing Good Deeds for store clerks when he should be looking for a job.

"Uh, I don't suppose there's an opening for a job in this store," he said.

"No," she said, shaking her head firmly. "No, there isn't."

Heck felt like he should apologize, but he was having

trouble remembering what he'd said.

"You wouldn't want to work here," she said. "The pay is terrible."

"I only need enough money to make a phone call." What was he talking about? What phone call?

She pulled some change out of her pockets. "Here," she said.

"No, no, I didn't mean ..."

"Take it. The phone's over there." She poured the change into his hand and turned away.

"If you need me, Jennifer, just call," Heck said, and he left the store. He glanced back once. She was watching him.

Wow. That was super-nice of her. He hoped he'd made her day a little better, but he had to move on. There were no apartment-sized Good Deeds to be found in an orderly men's clothing store. He shrugged his shoulders, shoulders that felt unusually strong today.

He felt good, like the whole world was made for him, like nothing could be taken away. His flat life seemed like a dream, a place where nothing was solid, where he couldn't grab on to anything, couldn't change anything, couldn't stop anything from dying. Now he was round enough to do whatever it was he had to do—save his mom, even. Now his teeth didn't hurt at all.

Heck noticed two boys counting their change at a popcorn vendor. One of them asked the girl at the counter, "Can you give us half a bag for this much?"

The girl behind the counter had seven earrings in each ear,

two in her eyebrow, one in her nose, and one in her lip. She didn't answer them, didn't look at them.

"Girl? Girl, can we buy half a bag for half the money?" the other boy asked.

She looked at them and shook her head slowly. "No half bags allowed," she said. She had a ball bearing pierced into her tongue. Behind her the popcorn popper came to life. Heck wondered if she could make electrical machines operate just by willing them to. She'd be able to do it because of the magnetic field created by all the metal in her face.

He stepped up to the counter just as the boys turned away disappointed. "Wait," he said to the boys. To the girl he said, "May I have two bags of popcorn, please?" He placed the change the clerk had given him on the counter.

Without answering she snapped open a bag and began filling it languidly. The boys smiled at each other. "You don't have to," one boy said to Heck.

"Yes. Yes, I do," Heck said soberly.

The girl put the bags on the counter and scooped the change off the counter. "That'll be four dollars."

Heck handed the popcorn to the boys. "Run along now," he said.

"Thanks!" they said in unison.

"They don't look like they're starving to death to me," the girl said, counting the change. She counted again. "Four dollars. You're missing a dollar."

"Are you sure?"

"I'm sure."

Heck felt his superface blush. "I will pay you the rest another day," he said. "Until then, if you need help, just call. The name's Heck."

"Yeah, whatever. That's funny. You're still a dollar short."

"I could give you some advice," Heck offered. "With all the metal in you, it's possible it is reacting with radiation leaking from that machine. If you start developing a strange growth out of the side of your neck that appears to be a second head—"

She flipped open a cell phone. "I'm calling security," she said.

Mutant–human relations had never been good.

He left the mall to walk the streets of Metropolis among the beautiful skyscrapers, built for people who could fly. Now that he'd given his money away, he remembered what he'd needed it for: to call Dierdre.

That was okay. Everything was okay. He'd walk there. He was feeling like he could walk all night.

Heck Superhero in the world of mortals, abandoned somehow in this dimension of weaklings without his super-suit, without the tokens of his strength—could feel himself fleshing out, feel his cricket quads, his butterfly lats layered over his adamantine skeleton. The streets were getting dark now, and filling with the shadows of the night people, but Heck could see as if it were day, past their shell faces and into the soft, moist being beneath. He could smell someone cooking chili miles away. Maybe it was Dierdre cooking for his mom, saying, Eat, eat, you're too thin. He could hear the cars draining out of the downtown, like water swirling out of a tub, and then a sucking sound, and then silence.

The in-between people had gone.

Now there were the million-dollar penthouse people and the people who slept under trees and on park benches. Now there were the BMWs and the shopping carts; the ones who had memberships to fitness clubs and the ones who walked all day; the ones who dined out and the ones who dined outside. Now there was the topworld and there was the bottomworld.

Heck loved them all, and why shouldn't he, muscled up as he was, powered up, coming off the page, shoulders above his chin, layered chest, narrow four-paneled abdomen. Why shouldn't he love them, his poor mortal mother among them, when he could see that they must live here under the shadowed towers of Metropolis, in one time and one dimension, and all the evil on the streets hiding in cracks and holes.

Heck moved in frames now, one frame to another, like in a comic strip, and under his feet were words leading him to his destiny as a force for good in the world. He remembered he was supposed to be going to Dierdre's, but he'd forgotten where that was.

Heck Superhero, sensing an opportunity to do a Good Deed, slipped into a laundromat.

No one was in the laundromat, but someone had left her laundry tumbling in the dryer. Could they be his mom's clothes? Was she here doing her laundry? No. He'd see jeans and T-shirts and waitress uniforms if the clothes were his mom's.

The dryer stopped a moment later.

If they had been his mom's, it would have made her happy if he folded them for her. He pulled the clothes out. Some person would return after a long day and find her work done.

He was just trying to figure out how you folded a bra when a lady walked in. The way she stopped short, surprised, told him that the clothes' owner had returned. Heck put the bra on top of the folded clothes like a cherry on a sundae. "No thanks necessary, ma'am," he said.

"Pervert," she said. She spun around and walked out.

Heck left the laundromat. She'd gotten into her car and locked the doors. She was talking on a cell phone. Likely she'd spend the night with a police artist, making a composite drawing of his face.

Heck walked away lightly so his feet wouldn't crack the sidewalk. How could he expect people to understand? They were only bottomworld feeders, trapped in one space and one time and so soft and vulnerable.

The whole city had gone anime. Buildings leaned over like wilting flowers and some disappeared at the edges, as if only the suggestion of a city were necessary. The roads shrugged and stretched as if they were just waking up.

He hoped his mom wasn't walking around the streets at night, alone, among the bottomworld dwellers. She was so small, so breakable. No, she would be at Dierdre's. That was it: Dierdre's.

But what if Dierdre had a no-weekday-sleepovers policy like at Spence's? He had to keep moving, had to keep the streets safe for breakable mothers everywhere.

Heck could hear whispers in the dark, then the sound of running feet. He'd come to a high plywood fence surrounding the crater of a construction site. He saw that he'd frightened off a couple of kids, and they'd left behind a spray can of black paint.

He picked up the can and drew a cityscape rising from the ground like building blocks. He spotted his blacks and began on the foreground detail. He peeked in the windows he drew, looking for an empty apartment that would be good for him and his mom. They didn't need much—a bedroom for her, he could sleep on the couch. He looked for his mom, too, in the cityscape. Dierdre's—she'd be at Dierdre's.

"Hey, that's good," someone said behind him.

There were some kids standing there looking at him when he turned around.

"You want to hang with us?" the tallest one said.

"Come on, Beemer," one of them said. "Leave him alone."

"Come on, kid. Wanna have some fun?" Beemer said.

"No," Heck said. He had work to do, good to uphold, evil to destroy. He put the paint can down.

Beemer grabbed him by the back of the jacket. Beemer must have downloaded his soul into a cyborg shell or he wouldn't have been so inhumanly strong, wouldn't have been able to shake him.

"Leave me alone, Cyborg," Heck said.

Beemer looked at the others and then at Heck again. "Are you some kind of freak or something?"

"No," Heck said.

Beemer turned to the others. "He says he's not a freak." He gave Heck another good-natured shake, and Heck's head flipped back as if his neck were boneless.

"I'm not a freak, I'm a superhero."

No one moved or said a word. Their eyes slid between Heck and Beemer. Finally Beemer laughed and said, "I'd like to see Mr. Hero here leap off a tall building or something, wouldn't you, brothers?"

Heck's thoughts raced at superspeed. What Good Deed could get him out of the death grip of a cyborg?

Then he knew: Donate his jacket!

Quick as a flash Heck's arms were out of his jacket sleeves.

Speedlines!

The cyborgs called after him as he ran away, but no one chased him. They must have known they'd never be able to catch him.

Maybe Dierdre's was too far away after all. He'd call. Except when he put his hand in his pocket, he realized he didn't have that change anymore.

His tooth was hurting again. His magnificent, powered-up

body was shrinking. Every superhero had his Achilles' heel, his weakness. Heck had his teeth. He headed for his old apartment building.

The moon was setting by the time he arrived and it was cold outside. When he arrived, just to be sure, he crept into the building and tried his key in the lock of his ex-apartment, just as he'd done the night before.

It still didn't work.

He went out back to the parking lot, to Mr. Hill's 1958 Thunderbird. Heck thanked the forces for good in the universe that he'd remembered the old man never drove it and never locked it. He could hear people laughing across the street, and someone said the name Beemer. Heck heard a strange whistling sound. He listened closely, but then all was silent.

From a trash can he took some paper, and on it he wrote with his trusty pencil, "Will fight evil for food." In smaller print he wrote, "Discount on Good Deeds."

"Stop it," he said to himself.

But he couldn't stop. Not yet.

Maybe in a minute.

He propped the sign on the windshield and climbed into the car.

When it began to rain, Heck imagined that the car was moving. Someone in the front seat was driving him somewhere, to a picnic maybe. Someone was going to lean over the front seat and say, It's okay, go back to sleep. He dreamed that in the trunk of the car there was fried chicken and potato salad and chocolate cake, all for him, Heck Superhero.

Heck woke up cold.

He lay there, following the filament of electric pain from the nerve in his tooth, into his jaw, down his neck and spinal cord, and back up to his brain. Where was his jacket? Bad dreams swirled like galaxies in the space in his head.

He opened his eyes. A bad dream had opened the car door and was looming over him—a big kid, older than him and wearing a navy pea jacket. "Five," the bad dream said.

"What ... ?"

The dream had a big, round, smooth head and a soft tuft of blondish hair. "Five, five!" he insisted. Heck rubbed his eyes, but the kid didn't go away. "That means 'Help,'" the kid whispered, somewhat exasperated. He stuffed something into Heck's pocket. "I didn't kill the squirrel. The cyborgs did. I just wanted to give it a decent burial." He glanced behind him, then ducked away.

Heck sat up slowly. The kid had stuffed a five-dollar bill into his pocket.

Heck saw a police car parked on the side of the street opposite the parking lot. From a hole in a landscaped lawn of an office building a man in overalls pulled a small furry body while the officer looked on. They talked together a moment.

Heck studied the five-dollar bill. It looked real enough. Then he saw the sign he'd written.

He jumped out of the car, ripped up the sign, and stuffed the pieces into his pocket with the fiver. He shut the door and pulled his hood over his head. His head felt so flat it was a miracle he had anything to hook his hood onto. He remembered the girl at the popcorn machine. It wasn't a bad dream. He made a mental note to give her the buck he owed her. He remembered the woman in the laundromat, too. What had he been thinking?

The pill. Velocity Nine. So that was what this stuff was all about. He was a thief and a garbage-eater and now a druggie, and for sure one crayon short of a full box.

Only a week ago he'd been an almost ordinary student in grade eight, so almost ordinary he could fool most people into thinking he was normal. Now he was waking up in a car with a dry mouth and glue for spit and his teeth sprouting fur.

Suddenly the officer shouted and took off across the street after the boy who'd stuffed the fiver into Heck's pocket.

The boy stopped when he saw the officer coming. He rounded his shoulders and waited, hunched and braced and clutching at his coat. The officer said something to him, took the boy's arm, and led him toward his car.

The boy was taller than the officer, but he had a babylike body, roundish and topped by that big ball of a head with its smooth cheeks. He wrapped his arms tightly around himself and glanced at Heck with a pained expression.

"It's not like you to damage property," the officer said to the boy. "Have you been taking your pills?"

"I didn't do it," the boy said.

"Who did, then? Your little pocket buddies? We're going to have to wash that coat for sure this time, Marion."

The boy's bottom lip pushed out, but he didn't answer. He looked as if he might cry. Heck couldn't stand to see a kid cry, even a kid that big. The kid cast a long, sad look at him, and Heck realized he'd been paid five dollars for a Good Deed. He sure did need that five dollars. He sure was hungry.

He cleared his throat. He could keep the cash and walk away, but that wasn't what superheroes did, even flat ones.

"Excuse me," Heck called.

The officer glanced at him and away.

"Um, did you consider the possibility that you've got the wrong guy there?" Heck called.

The officer stopped. His expression was stony, while the boy's face was slack with surprise and relief.

"Yeah?" the officer said, squinting at Heck.

What was he doing? His tooth throbbed. A toothache was something that could drag you back to the microverse where you were just a stupid kid who made a stupid sign when he was high on a birth control pill. He cleared his throat again. "What are the charges?" he asked.

The officer peered at him as though he had x-ray vision and could see Heck's guilty heart. "I hadn't thought of charges," he said slowly, "but let's see—digging a hole in private property, that would be a good start. And of course the SPCA will definitely have something to say about that dead animal. "

"It was dead when I found it ... I just wanted to give the squirrel a decent—" The kid slapped his hand over his mouth.

The officer smirked and Heck rolled his eyes. "The real crime is the squirrel, right? Sir?"

The officer said to the big kid, "I didn't know you had any friends."

The kid said nothing. He looked down at his shoes and then stole a grateful glance at Heck.

Heck tried to look at the officer in a respectful way without being too challenging. It was obvious the birth control pill hadn't quite worn off yet, because here was proof: he was being a complete billiard ball brain.

On the other hand, who owned reality? Maybe if he helped this kid he'd get more than five bucks out of it. Maybe something good would happen, like finding his mom.

"I know who did it. I heard his friends call him Beemer."

The officer looked at him and nodded. "Oh? You a friend of Beemer's?"

"No, but I heard them. They—they took my jacket."

The officer hesitated, then let go of the boy. With a look of disgust at Heck, he jerked his thumb toward his car. "Okay. You seem to know so much. Come on."

The boy walked away fast, whispering to himself.

Heck was hungry and dizzy and cold. Maybe they'd have

doughnuts at the cop shop, he thought. Didn't they always have doughnuts? He'd always wanted to ride in a cop car. Once he was in, though, he was nervous. What would Spence say when he found out that his molecularly joined best friend had become an outlaw, a public enemy, a wrongdoer of the bottomworld? And what about his mom? If he were in prison, she'd go into hypertime and never come back.

The police joked with Heck. They wrote down his name and address—he gave them the old one—and fingerprinted just his thumb. Then they put him in a room alone.

"Is this an interrogation room?" Heck asked.

"An interview room," the officer said.

Heck sat there a long time, but no one came to interview him. Nothing was in the room but a table, a chair, and a clock. Maybe they called it an interview room, but Heck knew a jail cell when he saw one. There were no windows, and nothing to read and nothing to look at. The only sound was the clock. It didn't tick. It hummed, pleased with itself, until the eleven. The hum turned into a moan as the minute hand went from the eleven to the twelve, as if it couldn't bear to begin again.

Heck wondered who had decided how long a second was, and who decided how many seconds made a minute. Who thought up how long an hour was so there were twenty-four of them in a day? Why not twenty hours in a day, or seventeen, or thirty-three? Why not just three—a day hour, an evening hour, and a night hour? His mom would probably be able to handle that.

You couldn't sit in a room with a clock like that and not want to go into hypertime. Reality time was thick in that room. It was speaking to him. Heck? Oh, He-eck, are you there? It's not working. You tried the Good Deed and look where it got you.

"It works," Heck said out loud. It was the Theory of Everything. The day he stuck up for Jasper Hillman against school villain Chris Vander was the same day he found his best friend, Spence. Spence said no, they'd been working up to it a long time, but Heck knew what he knew. Just last week he got the top grade in math class. Why? Because he helped Jenny Mellancamp with her math homework that day at lunch. The Good Deed was the only way to change the reality you were in right now, the only way to make everything okay.

When he thought about it, though, the clock had a valid argument. He found a lost little girl, and a security guard memorized his face for future criminal identification. He gave a girl a twenty, and she started him on a lifetime of addiction. He tried to be a hero, and he ended up here on death row. Still, there was a certain cool factor in becoming a villain ...

It's not working, the clock said. You have to stop playing.

Heck's dreams floated in his head flat as photographs: him graduating, going to art college, eating tortillas every Sunday, his pockets full of freshly ironed money. None of them would happen now that he was an official young offender, a wrongfully convicted evildoer, an accused villain spoiler of perfectly landscaped private property. The photograph dreams floated sideways and Heck couldn't see them anymore.

He took out his trusty pencil and a piece of the torn paper in his pocket. He sketched a superhero, powered up, ready to spring. It was a small piece of paper, so it didn't take long. He drew another one. If pretending he was a superhero who went about doing Good Deeds was his favorite game, drawing superheroes was a close second. As he drew, he remembered that Einstein's theory of relativity proved that there is no such thing as a universal clock, no absolute time.

After a few more minutes, his teeth didn't hurt as much. Probably they were starving to death, and he hoped they would die before he did.

When he'd sketched both sides of all the pieces of paper, he began to pace. He had to get out of here and call Dierdre. He had to tell his mom all the reasons why she was the best mom in the world. He had to get a job and tell her he could take care of her, before she killed all her hopes and went through hypertime into who knows what microverse.

He called, "Is anybody out there? Can I have a doughnut?"

A few minutes later the handle rattled and a man came in. He was wearing gray pants and a beige shirt and his eyes were gray and his face was beige and his hair was no particular color at all. Heck could barely perceive his outline against the cinderblock walls and the gray tiled floor. His face was settled into a bland, benign expression. He slipped a manila file onto the small table.

"Hello, Hector," he said.

"Heck," said Heck.

"I'm Mr. Holland." He took in the scrap-paper sketches.

"You're pretty good, Hector," he said.

The man was wearing a plain, dull silver wedding band on his ring finger. Heck imagined the man had been married for a long time. Maybe he and his wife had tried for years to have children and then for years tried to adopt, and one day they began thinking how they were too old to start with babies ...

"They say you gave yourself up concerning the buried squirrel."

Heck nodded. Gave himself up. That had a noble ring to it. "I didn't do it. Beemer did. It was me in the Underwear Incident, though," he said.

The man looked puzzled. "Underwear incident?"

"The woman who called from the laundromat last night about someone folding her laundry for her?" Heck sat back in his chair and pointed at his chest. "That was me."

The man opened the file. His face did not change, did not register shock, anger. He would probably be a very patient father. Too bad about his wife, who had tragically died two years ago, and only now Mr. Holland was beginning to think about remarrying ... someone small ... with a single older child ... a son ... the son he'd always dreamed of having ...

"That's very honest of you, Hector—"

"Heck."

"—and so for your honesty we've decided to let you go this time." He didn't look at Heck when he said it. He was leafing through the file, reading it.

"You mean you're not going to arrest me?" Heck's head swam with relief.

"Not this time, Hector." Mr. Holland smiled. "We think you're just covering for your friend anyway."

"That kid?"

The man nodded. "We've had ... dealings with him."

Heck was pretty sure he could smell a toasted Western sandwich somewhere.

The man found something in the file. He read in silence for a moment. All his movements were measured, controlled, his voice perfectly modulated. He probably made good money at this job. He'd give Heck's mom a good home, and Heck would get his own room.

"It says here your mother dropped you off at a crisis daycare when you were four and didn't come back for a few weeks. You spent a little time in a foster home."

They had a file on him! "Does the FBI have access to that file?" Heck asked.

Mr. Holland continued speaking, more to himself than to Heck. "In a follow-up interview, a social worker found that at seven years of age you could cook oatmeal, macaroni, pancakes, and scrambled eggs. At nine, you did the laundry, cleaned the house, signed your own permission forms, and got yourself off to school every day. It seems you excelled in all subjects." He closed the file. "Still doing well?"

Heck nodded shyly. Of course, a man who blended in with cinderblock would want a son who got good marks in school.

"We'll have to call your mom to come and get you. It appears that the number we have here is an old one, out of service. What's the new number?"

"Well, it's just that ..." Heck's throat flattened then and nothing came out. He was a thief, a druggie, an almost-convicted vandal. Was he going to be a rat now, a kid who would rat on his own mom? "She's not home right now." Even while he said it he thought he should tell. *Knew* he should tell.

"Do you know her work number?"

Heck shook his head and stared at his sketches. Mr. Holland was a good guy. Tell him. Tell him ...

The man picked up a scrap-paper sketch, examined it, and put it back down again. "You know, Hector—"

"Heck."

"—there are some kids who, even in the worst kind of circumstances—"

" My mom is cool, it's just that—"

"—seem to thrive and channel their experience into their talents. You're one of them. In the social-work biz we call them 'superkids.' That's another reason why I'm going to make this as simple as possible."

Heck held on to his chair so he wouldn't fall off. Superkid?

The man kept talking, but Heck didn't hear a word he said.

"Did you say 'superkid'?" Heck interrupted. The man nodded.

Once in a while in the world, didn't everything fall into place?

Once in a while, didn't the whole world make sense?

"Hector, it comes down to this: we have big problems around here, so I'm just going to send you home and recommend you be grounded for a year or two, okay? So, what's your number?"

Well, if he was only dreaming, well, then. If he was living in his comic book dream he could do anything. He could leap over tall buildings in a single bound, he could tell time in all realities, and he could find his mom and take care of her.

"Number, Hector?"

A superhero was always honest.

Heck told him the number.

"You playing straight with me, Hector? That number's been disconnected."

"She hasn't paid the bill in a while."

"Oh." Mr. Holland leaned back in his chair. "Are you sure everything's okay at home?"

"Sure," Heck said. "Uh, you could call Mr. Bandras. He's my art teacher at school."

Mr. Holland left the room to make the call. Heck got down and did twenty pushups. Cons had to stay fit while they were in solitary confinement. Of course he knew Mr. Bandras would come. Mr. Bandras was always willing to get into Heck's business, always trying to get into his mind.

"What does this mean to you, Heck?" he would ask when Heck was done with an art piece. "What were you thinking here? What feeling were you trying to portray here?" Those were the worst questions. It wasn't quite as bad when he asked Heck what he'd eaten for breakfast, or what he was having for lunch. Once or twice a week, when Heck "forgot" his lunch, Mr. Bandras would say, "Thank the Fates. Mrs. Bandras packed me bologna (or peanut butter or ham and cheese) sandwiches again and she knows I hate bologna (or peanut butter or ham and cheese)." Then he would toss his lunch at Heck. It embarrassed Heck, the way Mr. Bandras made a point of buying his art supplies for him when he couldn't come up with them himself.

Once Heck complained about it to Spence, but Spence said Mr. Bandras was only like that with Heck, and he should be grateful.

It was true that everything he knew about art he'd learned from Mr. Bandras. Especially the one thing. After a few classes with Mr. Bandras, Heck had been trying to copy something exactly, drawing it just right. People always admired him for the way he could draw things exactly. Mr. Bandras, however, had come up behind him and grabbed the pencil out of his hand.

"You are a talented boy," he said, "but we have cameras for that. Besides, you will try all your life to draw things exactly as they are, and discover you can't draw anything the way it really is. You can only draw it the way *you* really are."

When he said that, Heck felt like someone had just added an extra room to the house of his brain. That's when he knew that reality was just clay, something you could mold, or paint, or change by doing Good Deeds.

He could hear voices through the cinderblock walls but not what the voices were saying. After a long time a girl in a uniform brought Heck a sandwich and a juice cup.

"Do you like tuna?" she asked.

A long time ago, like last Sunday, he hated tuna. "Love it," he said.

He lifted the top piece of bread and examined the tuna. She frowned. "Just looking for truth serum," he said to her.

It was almost four o'clock by the time he heard Mr. Bandras's voice talking to the beige and gray man. They talked a long time, and then the door opened.

Mr. Bandras was not beige and gray. He was not mild-mannered. He had red hair and a red face that got redder when he talked about great artists. He wore a garish tie every day to remind his students, he said, of the "assault on the eye that constitutes bad art." His jeans and shirt were always smeared and splattered with bright paint. Heck thought he had never seen a more beautiful sight in his life than that ugly tie.

He stood up and swayed on his feet.

Mr. Bandras glanced at the sketches and then at Heck and then at the sketches again.

"Let's go," he said.

As they walked out, the beige and gray man said, "Bye, Hector. Be good now, okay?"

Heck nodded and then stopped. "I'm sorry about your wife and, you know, about you not being able to have kids and all."

"My wife is fine, and I have kids," Mr. Holland said.

"Oh," Heck said. "Sorry. I must have you confused with some other CIA agent."

"Come on, Heck," Mr. Bandras said.

For a long time Mr. Bandras said nothing to Heck as he drove him to the apartment building. He'd driven Heck home before when he had artwork that was too big to take on the bus.

The teacher listened to classical music and drummed on the steering wheel as if it were rock music. Heck was pretty sure he was trying to torture him. Mr. Bandras had probably once been your average run-of-the-mill art teacher, until one day he was visited by parasitic robots from a distant and hostile world. It had been his desire, since then, to bring sorrow and suffering to all junior high art students of the mortal world. Still, it felt good to be freed from prison.

Mr. Bandras switched off the radio. "So, Heck, why weren't you at school today, instead of getting into trouble?" Mr. B. didn't look all that happy.

"I was sick. It was a stomach thing," Heck said. That was almost true.

"That's why taxpayers pay for school toilets," Mr. B. said.

Nope, Heck thought, Mr. B. was not happy, not happy at all.

"You need to be at school, Heck, not out digging graves for small furry animals."

"Yes, sir."

"Was it a stomach thing yesterday?"

"No, sir, I had a ... rash."

"A mess of plagues at your house, isn't there?" Mr. B. said. His face was getting redder.

"Sir, your blood pressure ..."

"If you're concerned about my blood pressure, don't make me have to pick you up at police stations!"

Heck didn't answer. He decided he would not rescue Mr. B. when aliens abducted the man to perform their fiendish experiments on him.

"You haven't got it easy, Heck. I know that. But you're not the only kid in the world who's had it tough. Skipping school and getting into trouble is no way to make it better."

"Yes, sir," Heck said, but he was thinking Mr. B. didn't really understand the situation. He had to rescue his mom out of hypertime. The longer she was there, the closer he got to the dimension of Your Mom Is Gone.

"You're thinking I don't really understand, aren't you?" Mr. B. said.

Some kind of mind-meld trick.

"I do understand," Mr. B. continued. "I understand that skipping school is *selfish*. And getting into trouble like this is *selfish*. How will your mom feel when she finds out where you've been today? And she will find out, because I'm going to tell her."

Heck's head suddenly felt too heavy for his spindly neck. He couldn't figure out why, since his head was obviously pretty empty and shouldn't weigh too much. Mr. B. was right. The worst thing in the world he could do would be to get himself in trouble. That would push him closer to the dimension of Your Mom Is Gone for Good.

"Yes, sir," he said. "I'm sorry, sir."

Mr. B. must have been able to hear the acknowledgment of idiocy in his voice, because the teacher's voice was a lot softer when he spoke again.

"You've been drawing superheroes again," Mr. B. said. "Every time things are out of control for you, you start drawing superheroes and you stop producing artwork."

Heck felt his face flush all the way down to the three hairs he had recently sprouted on his chest. True. All true.

"Comic art is artwork," he protested weakly.

Mr. B. ignored him. "One day I see you drawing superheroes, later I find out you flunked your math test that day. Another day I see you drawing superheroes, and come to find out you and Spence are on the outs. Next day you two are best buddies again, and you start producing this artwork. Okay, it's astigmatic—"

"What does that mean?" Heck asked.

"You factor the earth's axis into everything you draw. But I'm going to tell you something, Heck. I've been teaching for twenty-four years. For twenty-four years I've been telling myself that my work is meaningful, that I've been enriching the lives of children by introducing them to the soul-expanding visual arts. Maybe I've done that. But some of the kids I taught my first year are turning thirty-seven this year. They are clerks and salesmen and mechanics and doctors. None of them go to art galleries, never mind pick up a paintbrush. Sometimes they dazzle their kids and draw a really good horse. Are you hearing me, Heck? If I had a nickel for every time a student came back and said, 'Thanks for enriching my life with the visual arts,' I'd have a whole fifteen cents. I've spent fifty-one thousand eight hundred and forty hours of my diabetic and therefore shortened lifespan babysitting art students."

He pulled up and parked in front of Heck's ex-apartment building. He sighed. "Then you came along, Heck. Once in a lifetime a student like you. Someone with art eyes. It was worth twenty-four years to get you. Now, I know you, and I know something's going on."

Tell him. Tell him, tell him, tellhim tellhim tellhimtellhimtell—

"Everything's okay. Thank you, sir."

"You need money? You got groceries at home? Off the record. No one but me has to know."

"We're fine, sir." Heck climbed out of the car carefully. If he bumped his head all the air in there would leak out, creating a vacuum. "Thanks, Mr. B.," he said. He meant it. Thank you, Mr. B., for bringing me to my senses, or my knees, or maybe both because my sense is in my knees ...

Mr. Bandras got out, too. "I'll go in with you, Heck, leave a note for your mom."

Heck's heart screamed, causing his kidneys to faint and his bladder to give up the ghost. Fortunately there was nothing in his system but tuna sandwich. "No," Heck said as calmly as he could. "You'd better not come in. The place is saturated with germs, big juicy germs. I told you, I've been sick. Don't I look sick?" Heck tried to look as sick as he could. It wasn't hard, since it was making him feel a bit sick to lie, and since the bacteria in his teeth were dining on his juicy tooth pulp with pointy forks and knives.

"You look terrible." Mr. Bandras considered Heck for a moment. "Remember, Heck, when you told me about ... about that comic book artist—what was his name?"

"Oh, yeah, that guy," Heck said. Leave, he was thinking. Please just leave.

"Remember you told me he was one of the greats? That he was an innovator in the way comics are drawn?"

Heck stopped nodding. "You mean Will Eisner?"

"That's it. Eisner."

"You remember me telling you about him?" Heck asked.

"Of course I do. You told me that everything used to be drawn inside the panels. This Eisner was the first to break outside the borders."

Heck was impressed. "Pretty good memory for someone your age," he said.

Mr. Bandras spoke over him. "That's right. Will Eisner. You be like him, Heck. You do a little border-breaking of your own. You know what I mean?"

"Yes, sir." He did know what he meant. He meant not to be framed in by people's low expectations of him. He meant for Heck to be bigger and better than what the picture said right now.

Mr. B. relaxed. "You have an assignment due tomorrow.

Self-portrait. No superhero stuff. You'll be in school tomorrow, right?"

"I should be," he said. Yes, he should be.

Mr. Bandras nodded curtly. "No superheroes. Self-portrait."

Heck nodded.

"All right. And if you're not at school, I'm coming to your place to check on you." Before he got back in the car he pointed. "And don't forget, the semester portfolio is due Friday," he said.

Heck waved as Mr. Bandras drove away. It was Tuesday. He had three days before he had to tell Mr. B. that all his work was gone. It was probably being sold on the homework black market at this very minute.

He felt guilty. Guilty for lying and guilty for not going to school. Maybe his mom had worked something out. He needed to call Dierdre, but he'd given his change away for popcorn. Why had all his Good Deeds gone for naught? Was he somehow trapped in a negative zone, heading for a life of hard-boiled crime? Had he swapped souls with his diametric double and become trapped in a world where Good Deeds only had bad outcomes?

Then he remembered the five dollars that boy had shoved in his pocket.

He pulled it out and gazed at it.

Wow.

It was all okay.

The Forces for Good in the world were alive and well.

He bought a Happy Meal and gave his toy to the first child he saw. Then he phoned Dierdre.

It rang a long time. On the last ring Heck remembered she worked the night shift at the casino and she'd be sleeping.

"Hello?" she mumbled.

"Dierdre? Dierdre, it's me, Heck."

She dropped the receiver and picked it up. "Who's dead?"

"Dead? Someone's dead?" Heck said, his heart going from zero to light speed.

"I'm asking. What time is it?" He heard her light up a cigarette.

"It's almost five-thirty. I wouldn't have called, but I really need to talk to my mom."

Dierdre yawned. "She's not here, buddy."

Heck felt the spin in every one of the elementary particles of his brain. "Not ... there?"

Dierdre slammed the receiver three times on something hard, then came back on the line. "Echo in my phone," she muttered.

Heck changed ears. His spit was the consistency of goo. "Well, have you seen her lately?"

"Yeah. She was over yesterday. Wait a minute—you mean she hasn't come home yet?"

Heck didn't answer and Dierdre didn't fill up the silence.

"Hypertime, I think," Heck said finally, low and soft.

Dierdre swore, but at least all the sleep was gone from her

voice. "I should have known. She didn't talk much, just said a couple of times what a great kid you were ..."

"Did she stay overnight?"

"No. I sent her home, told her she shouldn't leave you alone like that in the apartment." Dierdre sucked on her cigarette like she was dying for breath and there was a superior form of oxygen in there. She swore again.

"Dierdre, do you think she'd be with that guy she went out with a while ago? She told Levi to forward her check there."

"You never know what she's gonna do. Are you okay, though? I'm going to call the cops if you're not okay."

"Mom would hate that."

"Okay. I'll wait a day. You call me tomorrow and we'll talk. You got milk and bread in the house? Listen, I'll come by with some groceries, okay?"

"I'm okay, Dierdre. Everything's okay."

Dierdre understood maybe even better than Heck about his mom, how she was a good mom, she just had this hypertime issue sometimes when things weren't okay. Sometimes, when people found out about Heck and his mom, they judged her. But Dierdre knew his mom would never enter the dimension of Evil Motherhood. She went instead to the dimension where you got to be a little girl and wear watches that never said it was time to grow up.

He looked at the money left in his hand. Which would make him feel better, a chocolate bar or phoning Spence?

He dialed Spence's number.

Spence picked up the phone quickly. "Why weren't you in school again today?"

"I was in jail," Heck said. "Solitary confinement and no doughnuts."

"Yeah, where all truants end up, but usually not so fast. You're joking, right?"

"It was a case of mistaken identity," Heck said, which was almost true.

"So, seriously, are you sick or something?"

"Flat," Heck said.

"Again?"

"Still." He knew what the answer was going to be, but he asked anyway. "I don't suppose my mom called?"

"Your mom?"

"You know, the birth parent?"

Spence said, "Why would she phone for you here on a school night?" After a pause he said, his voice lowered, "You mean—are you supposed to be staying at my house? Is that why she phoned Sunday night?"

Heck reached into his pocket and fingered his sketching pencil.

"Speak!" Spence said. After a moment he said, "I mean it, Heck! If—if you want me to be your friend, you'd better spill."

Heck had to tell him before he drowned in dark matter. "She probably thought the landlord was just trying to scare her when he kept giving her notice. She didn't even open the last couple. When I was at your house she came home and—and the locks were changed."

There was a long silence, a silence so deep it had suction to it.

Finally Spence said, "Why didn't you say something?"

"The no-sleepovers-on-school-nights policy," Heck said.

Spence spluttered, then screeched, "It didn't occur to you that this might be different?"

Heck could hear Spence's eyes going red-hole. Spence was the nicest guy in the world as long as his eyes didn't go red-hole. Heck admired pure mad. He could never unflatten his nerves enough to get that way, though.

"Okay, okay," Spence said, "so where have you been staying?"

"In the parking lot," Heck said. "Mr. Hill's '58 Thunder-bird."

No answer. "It isn't that bad," Heck said. "Hello?"

"What are you, hard-wired for self-destruction?" Spence said finally. "Why didn't you talk to me? I thought we were like, you know, acquaintances, you know, on speaking terms."

"I couldn't," Heck said. "What if it wasn't just one night? Which it wasn't. She said she'd call and she didn't. How long do you think I could stay there before your mom started asking questions? My mom's been in trouble before. People just don't understand how she and I work."

"I'm telling the police," Spence threatened.

"Sure. Get my mom arrested and I go to a group home and share a room with someone who crawls into my bed at night."

Spence said nothing. Heck could hear him gnawing on his fingernails, thinking. "It'll be bad for your mom, this whole apartment thing."

"Don't bite," Heck said. "Hey, man, everything's okay. I've got it all worked out." He loved it when Spence worried for him. It made him feel stronger. "The microverse is on my side."

"No. Please. Not that again." Spence swore. He had practiced swearing and now he was getting pretty good at it.

Heck raised his voice. "It works. You know it works every time."

"No, I don't know any such thing."

"Yes, you do."

"No."

"Yes!" Heck said. "Remember Jennie Abram and the fifty-dollar bill?"

"You know that was a fluke."

"You admitted yourself that shoveling Mrs. Tingle's walk brought that storm that closed the school."

"I was tired of arguing with you about it. I never did think they had anything to do with each other," Spence said. "And don't even mention the cat in the tree."

Heck didn't say anything. That was one of his favorites.

Finally Spence said, "So what should we do? You can't sleep outside and hang out all day. You'll end up in the Speed Force or something."

"Too late," Heck muttered to himself.

Spence was silent a moment. "What?"

"Nothing."

"*What did you say?*"

Heck said, "I'll never do it again."

After another silence, Spence said very calmly, "So you did the stupid thing, huh? You did Velocity Nine?"

Heck didn't answer.

"You've joined the stupid crowd, become one of the stupid."

"I know," Heck said. "I won't—"

"Didn't we talk about the Hi-Ho stupidity of that?"

"It's just that my teeth—"

"But don't worry," Spence said, his voice rising. "You're so smart you could become the Zen Guru of Stupid. You could become the Royal Emperor King of Stupid."

Heck let him yell himself out. When Spence took a breath, Heck said, "Wow."

"Wow?"

"Yes, wow. I mean, wow, thanks."

Spence said nothing.

"I mean, wow, that helped!" Heck said loudly. "That was just what I needed to hear. I'm cured. You could, you know, take that to the drug-addicted everywhere. Tell them they're stupid and they'll get their lives back on the straight and narrow. Tell them they're stupid and that'll help them get their act together and their heads on straight. They will forever give you the credit. You could, you know, start a rehab based on that. You could call it the Stupid Cure."

Heck was talking to a dial tone.

He slammed the phone down.

He'd show Spence. He was capable of taking care of himself. He'd get so topworld it would make Spence dizzy to look up at him.

No one could figure out why Spence hung out with Heck, never mind why they were best friends. Spence himself was probably wondering that right now. But maybe it was time to show Spence and the whole world that Heck was a power to be reckoned with.

Heck leaned against the phone.

Stop it. Spence was right. He was stupid. He should go talk to Spence's mom and trust her.

But. That would take care of food and where to sleep at night. It didn't solve the problem of his mom.

He would go to Spence's as soon as he found his mom. He'd ask the Carters to put them both up for a few days.

Think. Where would she go? Sam's? After he thought about it a minute, he decided no. Sam had wanted to get all serious, and his mom didn't feel that way. Sam would be her last resort. Where else? To a shelter or something? He'd heard in school about a shelter, but he didn't know where it was.

He walked the streets, looking for a shelter, or maybe someone who looked like he would know where it was. What would he say to her when he found her? Let's go stay at the Carters' for a while? No, she'd never go.

When he passed the Art Store he saw that it was still open, and the Help Wanted poster was still in the window. "Temporary gallery assistant required. Duties include facilitating installation of exhibition for Young Artists Contest. Also, assistance in coordination of events and help in developing strategies that will increase attendance. Could lead to permanent position."

Heck didn't really understand it, but he was pretty sure he could do it.

The Forces for Good in the world were at work.

"Successful applicant will have customer service skills and understand visual art practice."

That's me, Heck thought.

He stepped into the gallery and looked around.

A painting was the Good Deed on paper. A good painting, Heck believed, made the world worth saving. You could love a pot, or an old man, or a dirty window, or the color red if you looked at it enough to see it, and see it enough to paint it. With paintings, the world was as small as a canvas—you could just pick it up and kiss it.

"Can I help you?" A man with a ponytail approached him. His shirt was so baggy it hung on him like a robe. Still, he managed to look clean and well-groomed. Heck was suddenly aware that he probably looked anything but clean and well-groomed.

"I'm here to apply for the job of gallery assistant," Heck said. He had to enunciate clearly because his tongue was sticking to the roof of his mouth.

The man laughed. When Heck continued to gaze soberly at him, the man stopped laughing. "Well, sure," he said, "why don't you leave us your résumé."

"I don't have a résumé," Heck said, "but I got ninety-eight percent in Art last year."

"Last year in grade ... ?"

"Eight."

The man smiled. "What happened to the other two percent?"

"Room for improvement," Heck said. "My mom's taken me to art galleries before."

"Well, I think we're looking for someone a little older."

"I scrub toilets," Heck said.

The man nodded as if this were a curious thing, a matter of distinct interest.

"I need a job," Heck said. He swayed on his feet when he said it, as if the word "job" were big enough to bowl him over.

The man tugged on his ear. "I guess I have some cleaning that could be done around here before the contest."

"Can you pay me today?"

The man smiled. "So now he negotiates. Yes, I can pay you today, in cash. The cleaning gear is in the furnace room behind the bathroom."

Heck found the equipment. It was next to some shelving stacked with dust-covered art supplies. From a small, beat-up window in the furnace room Heck could see into the alley. He picked up some cloths and a blue spray bottle and began in the bathroom.

He cleaned the toilets, the sink, the taps, and the mirrors. He emptied the garbage and filled the paper-towel dispenser and mopped the floor. He tidied and swept the furnace room and the coffee room, and polished the microwave oven. He knew how to clean. His mom had worked as a cleaning lady for a while and sometimes she'd brought him along with her. On the wall in the coffee room was a poster about the high school art competition. He read it while he washed cups and spoons.

He vacuumed the main gallery area and surreptitiously examined the artwork. He loved the way some of the paintings opened up windows to other worlds. Others said there are no other worlds, this one is it, look at it, see it for what it is. Heck stopped for a moment and realized he was in the middle of a triangle of three paintings. The vacuum screamed at his side. They were all by the same artist, entitled One, Two, and Three. All three were of people running away from the viewer, from the artist, from the canvas. No full faces, just backs of bodies running into the paint. In each one, one person was glancing back in terror.

Heck took in a deep breath. He was too unround to cope with a flat world that said there was nothing to do but get sucked in.

The man turned the vacuum off.

"You like this?" he asked, nodding at the paintings. "All the art in here is by senior high school students. Very prestigious contest—the winner gets a full scholarship to the art college. There're second and third prizes of five thousand and one thousand dollars. Hey, the place hasn't looked this good in a while. Here. Thanks."

There were two crisp twenty-dollar bills. One for food and one for Spence.

"I run errands, too," Heck said.

"Okay. Sure."

"I noticed you have art supplies here," Heck said.

"Just a few old things in the back."

Maybe tomorrow he'd ask to work in exchange for art supplies. He could get a few things done to replace his lost portfolio. Which was due Friday. First, though, before he worried about the portfolio, he had to find his mom, tell her he had a job and she was a great mom and not to stay in hypertime because everything was okay.

"Do you happen to know where the shelter is?" Heck asked.

The man's expression changed. Heck wasn't sure if he was mad or sad. "No idea," he said.

Heck would find the shelter—tomorrow. It was a bit late, and he was tired. He was hungry, too, but even more tired than hungry.

He dreamed big dreams as he headed back to the '58 Thunderbird. He had a job now, but it had to be even better than that if he was going to take his mom all the way topworld. He couldn't stop thinking about the high school art competition. Maybe he would establish himself as a great artist, a child prodigy. He would win a full scholarship to art college. He would ... well, first he would make a painting that would be a Good Deed, yes, a painting that would banish tooth decay and cause landlords and best friends to come begging on bended knee.

All night long, sleeping in the old car, Heck dreamed he was running from flesh-covered cyborgs. He avoided lightning-flash punches and steel-toed kicks and flesh-burning lasers that melted mortal skin like butter. All night long he leapt from roof to roof until he couldn't run anymore. Then his mom was there, and he threw his arms around her, but it wasn't her. It was a hard-light hologram with her face.

When he woke up he was cramped and cold and sore. His teeth were itchy. Deep down in those black holes and down into the pulpy nerves and down past the nerve into the secret bone of his jaw it was itching. Not a nice tickly itch, but a buzzing bee-sting type of itch.

He sat up. Mr. Hill was peering at him through the window. He said something.

Heck rolled the window down. "Hey, Mr. Hill. Sorry about your car. I—I was just guarding it for you."

"You got any girlies in there with you?"

"No, sir. No girls."

Mr. Hill hit his cane on the ground. "Aren't you the boy

who lives upstairs?"

Heck smiled cordially. "Yes, sir. Used to. We've moved."

"Well, I don't like this. No sir. As for me and my car, we will serve the Lord, so you and your girl can just clean outta that car."

"Sir, I don't have a girl. See?" Heck lifted his feet and pushed up his sleeves. "I was just making sure no vagrants come and sleep in here at night."

"No girlies, eh? I was a boy once. I know how you think, what you're up to. But I've repented, and so's this car. Had it cleaned by professionals, had it blessed. Gonna be buried in it."

Heck got out of the car. It was another thing altogether to be sleeping in someone's coffin. "Sorry, sir, it won't happen again," Heck said.

"Better not. The world is coming to an end, son, and you can't hide your sins under a car top. Purify yourself, boy, prepare to meet the Lord. Stay your hand from the temptations of the flesh."

Heck's mom had taught him to be respectful of the elderly. "I didn't know you were a preacher, sir," he said, backing away.

"Wasn't. Broke every one of the Ten Commandments and a few the Lord forgot to mention. That's the beauty of getting old. Gives you cripple time to get yourself holy. But just in case you don't get old, take it from me, boy—"

"I won't," Heck said. "Anymore."

"Won't what?" He was having to raise his voice since Heck had gotten a distance away.

"Everything. Won't everything. I gotta go, sir." He did have to go to the bathroom. The old man started reciting something as Heck walked quickly away. Once he looked back, nodded, and waved.

Heck remembered his plan. Today he'd find the shelter. First, though, he'd walk to his job at the Art Store. He would work for canvas and paints, and make the painting that would establish him as a great painter. No. No, first he would make a portfolio to hand in so he wouldn't flunk Art. Also, he had to use the toilet.

The boy was watching him from a short distance away.

It was the boy he'd saved from an ignominious life in prison, the boy who'd shoved money into his pocket when he woke up yesterday. The boy was holding one side of his pea jacket open, as if he were going to reach into an inside pocket and pull something out. He was standing still like that, like half a flasher.

As he came closer Heck realized the boy was talking to the inside of his jacket.

"Fifty-five, fifty-five," the boy said to the inside of his jacket. He was tall and he had enormous feet. His face had a sweet, bland look to it. Heck could imagine a pacifier in his mouth.

"What?" Heck asked.

"Fifty-five. Friend or foe?" the boy said. Then he smiled. "The pocket creatures say 'friend.'" He must have gotten a dimple gene from both parents because he had dimples all over his face—one in each cheek, one up by his right eye, and a couple in his chin. "My name is Marion. Marion Ewald."

"Marion? That's a girl's name," Heck said.

"What's your name?" Marion asked.

"Heck."

"That's a swear. Heck what?"

"Heck Superhero," Heck said, hoping the boy would go away.

"I knew it," Marion said.

"Knew what?"

"I knew you were a superhero."

"Right."

"I did!"

"You've been probed," Heck said.

"Heck Superhero," the boy said. "I knew it." He sounded ... awed.

Heck stopped and looked closely at the boy. "Okay, so what was the tip-off?"

"The sign you wrote: 'Will Fight Evil for Food.' And also how you saved me from the police."

Heck looked at his feet. "Well, yeah, there is that."

"What else can you do?" Marion asked.

Heck shrugged. "Good Deeds."

Marion nodded solemnly and looked as if he were going to ask for Heck's autograph. He opened his jacket a little wider. "Five oh five five."

"Huh?"

"The pocket creatures say you're the one."

"The pocket creatures?"

"You're the one they trust to help release them."

"Did you say 'the pocket creatures'?"

"Yes. They come from the fifth planet. They traveled through space as spores and nested in my jacket and grew there. They're quite helpless. If I didn't protect them, they would die."

"I see," Heck said. He kept walking. This kid had definitely been probed. "So what do they eat?"

"Stardust," Marion said. "Or its earthly variation, pocket lint."

The boy followed him until he got to the Art Store. At the door Heck turned to him and said, "Look, I've got a job, and, um, I think they care who I hang out with."

Marion nodded. "I'll wait for you," he said.

Heck's bladder was too cramped up for him to argue. He went into the store.

The man with the ponytail seemed surprised to see him.

"Hello, sir, reporting for duty," Heck said, crossing his legs a little.

The man shuffled his papers as if he were looking for a work order, or a memo saying Heck had just passed the probationary period for 100% dental benefits.

"Should I start on the toilets?" Heck asked.

"Uh ..."

"Yesterday I noticed some litter around the dumpster, and there's a back alley window that needs repair."

"I'm afraid ... I don't have any cleaning work for you today," he said.

"Oh," Heck said. The cramp in his bladder had spread to his diaphragm and throat. "Well, maybe later, then. I'll drop by."

"I won't then, either. I'm sorry."

"Tomorrow?"

"No."

"Didn't I do a good job?"

"You did a great job, but it was just a one-time thing. Or maybe another time, but not every day, and not today."

"Well, have you filled the position for gallery assistant?"

"No, but ..." He sighed. "I need a grownup for that." He shrugged and shook his head. "I like to help out people like you, but sometimes you make it hard."

People like you. Heck couldn't think of anything to say, and his throat cramp wouldn't have let him speak anyway.

Marion of the pea-jacket pocket creatures was waiting for him when he burst out of the store.

"That didn't take long. Did you do it at superspeed?"

"No. I got fired."

"Big mistake to fire a superhero," Marion said.

Heck frowned, but suddenly he felt better. He headed to the mall to find a toilet. Marion followed him. "So, Marion, are you on major big drugs?"

"No. I don't do stuff like that. I don't smoke, either."

"I see."

"You think I'm crazy."

"I know it," Heck said.

"I'm not."

"Your word against overwhelming evidence," Heck said. It felt kind of good to have someone around to talk to, though, someone who believed in him, someone who ...

What was he thinking? Had a pocket creature spore entered his brain through his nose? Was it sitting on his cerebral cortex at this very moment, living off earwax and bites of brain stem? Never mind. Soon his teeth would start screaming and drive away all alien parasites.

"People tried to take my jacket away—the guidance counselor, the psychologist, even the one who says he's my father. They act like sleeping with your coat on is a federal offense." Marion lowered his voice and said, "They tried to give me pills, but the pills would have poisoned the pocket creatures."

Heck shook his head and snorted.

Marion stood still. "I believed you," he said.

"Did I ask you to? The superhero thing, it's just this weird game I play."

"A game is more fun if you believe," Marion said.

Heck thought about that. Besides, as he often reminded himself, in a quantum weird world, who has the only reality there is? He was just a kid who wanted to play, didn't want to hurt anyone, just wanted to help some helpless little space spores get back to their mommies. Good Deeds were seldom this easy. "Okay. Okay, I believe you," he said.

"No, you don't."

"Yes. I do."

"Why?"

"I'll tell you why: quantum theory." Heck crossed the street without waiting for a walk signal.

"Quantum ... what?"

"See, it's like this, Marion," he said as he walked. "In a quantum multiverse, every time you don't cross the street you create another microverse in which you do. There are other me's and you's wandering around in parallel microverses, all kinds of versions of Marion, and all possible variations of Heck. And maybe in one of those microverses little pocket aliens really exist. It's just that you can see that microverse, whereas most of us can't."

Marion smiled. "Do you mean that?" He had perfect teeth, Heck noticed.

"Well, sure."

Marion opened his jacket just a little and whispered to the inside pocket. Finally he said, "The pocket creatures say 'fifteen,' affirmative."

Heck walked faster.

One block to go. He could make it. His bladder was so cramped up now that nothing would come out when he got to the mall anyway.

"There's another reason why I know you're a superhero," Marion said.

"What's that?"

"Because you're not afraid of me."

The fluid buildup in Heck's body was making his gums swell, putting pressure on his teeth, which was turning the deep itch into hard, yellow-fingernail pinches. It was a wonder his teeth didn't pour blood out of those holes.

"Will you do another five-dollar Good Deed for me?" Marion asked.

"No," Heck said, "but if you're buying breakfast, I'll let you share with me."

"I'm not hungry," Marion said. He turned his headlight eyes on Heck. "I don't think I can release the spores all on my own. What if the cyborgs come, the ones that killed the squirrel? I just need someone to be there with me." He clamped his mouth shut on that.

"Maybe later," Heck said. Maybe he wasn't going to make it to the mall, to a toilet. Now he was walking so fast that he was leaving Marion behind.

"Fifth day? Fifth month?"

"Huh?"

"The fifth day of the fifth month," Marion called. "Their kind will come for them. Shh. Secret."

"Sure, Marion, sure." Heck was way ahead of him now. "Good-bye now. All the best to you and ... yours."

He could see the mall now. He could also see that he wasn't going to make it.

He turned into a driveway. He needed a corner. Just a corner.

He found a weedy corner in someone's yard just in time.

He was a water balloon. When all the water was out of him he collapsed into himself. The front parts of him and the back parts were stuck together. He felt himself folding against the wall.

Someone was staring at him. A man someone. A briefcase-and-suit someone. Heck didn't care. His stomach was still cramped up. The someone walked on and Heck stumbled away from the wall. He muttered, "Everything is ..." No, it wasn't exactly okay. He'd just peed outside. He didn't have a job. He needed to wash his hands. He needed a hot bath. *People like you* ...

He'd have to look for another job, that was all.

But what could a flat person do? You could hang him on two crossed sticks and tie on a string and he could be a kite. Or he could be a doormat, shoes licked for free.

If you were flat you could slide under locked doors at night and get stuff. Stuff you needed, like art supplies. When you were someone who urinated in public places it was the next logical step, wasn't it? If you were a person who stole money from your best friends and did drugs and went to prison, wasn't the next step to take stuff from people you didn't even know? If you urinated in people's driveways, that sealed it.

Heck's teeth had rhythm: *pain* pain pain *pain* pain pain ...

He punched his jaw.

Superheroes probably got fired all the time for having to take extra-long coffee breaks to save people. They probably threatened their superiors with their super-competence. He wasn't meant to clean toilets anyway. He was meant for higher things.

"Shut up, shut up," he told himself. He had to get a grip. Think.

He had to find the shelter. For sure his mom would be

there, getting deeper and deeper into hypertime. He had to have some good news to bring to her. Think.

He still had the money from working yesterday ...

The apartment building from which they'd been evicted had never seemed like much before, kind of run-down and saggy. Now he'd give a lot to see the kitchen picnic table that his mom had found in a park and that he'd painted like a picnic feast, complete with sandwiches and watermelon on the tabletop and ants crawling up the legs. He missed the color TV that they'd got secondhand and that was only a green-and-white TV. He even missed his mom's room, full of porcelain dolls and stuffed animals and pictures of kittens. Most of all he missed his own room that he'd converted into a sort of studio. If the Forces for Good were at work in the world, his paints would still be in that studio.

Heck thought back. When they'd first started getting notices from the landlord, Heck had tried staving off the inevitable with the power of the Good Deed. Without anyone knowing, he cleaned up the building sometimes. He swept the entranceway, or picked up bottles and garbage that people left in the halls or threw out the windows. Three nights before they'd been evicted, someone had vomited in the front entranceway. Heck had just stepped over it, probably at that moment sealing their Apartment Doom.

Heck stood before Apartment 1, where his landlord, Mr. Grenhold, lived. He could smell the cigarette smoke through the door. He could hear him coughing inside, a horrible cough, like he must be coughing up blood and tissue or giving birth to lung aliens through his mouth.

Heck breathed deeply a few times, willing his hand to lift up and knock on the apartment door, just lift up and knock ... Heck Superhero, afraid of nothing, knocked on the landlord's door.

When the landlord opened the door his bald head was dripping with sweat.

"What."

"Hey, Mr. Grenhold," Heck said cheerfully. "You may not remember me, but my mom was evicted last Saturday. I wondered if I could talk business with you, man to man. This twenty is a token of my good faith."

He held out the twenty. Mr. Grenhold took the money and scrunched it in his fist.

Mr. Grenhold had probably once been a mild-mannered retiree, living quietly in his apartment, until some intergalactic life form, perhaps inhabiting his refrigerator magnets, turned him into the boy-hating undead.

Heck cleared his throat. *Heck Superhero, afraid of nothing* ... "I promise I will repay you all the rent we owe, over time, if you'll just let me have my art supplies."

Mr. Grenhold started closing the door.

"Sir? Sir, have you noticed that the halls and stairways have been dirtier lately?"

The landlord opened the door again. "How'd you know that? You comin' in here at night and dropping garbage?"

"No, sir. It was me cleaning it up for you before, when I

lived here. Of course I did it as a part of my own personal philosophy of life, but now I was wondering if ... if we could work out some kind of arrangement."

"Crazy kid." Mr. Grenhold shut the door.

Heck knocked again, and then again a little while later. He could hear the landlord coughing, but he wasn't coming to the door. Heck decided to wait outside. He might have pushed it a bit far, telling him about the Good Deed. That had been the inspiration of the moment. When he came out, Heck would flash the other twenty and try to get just his paints.

He waited. He sat on a bench, a perfect place. Every so often he'd stand up and walk up and down the block, avoiding cracks in sidewalks and gratings. Then he'd sit on the bench again. Inertia: the slow but inexorable process by which boy and bench exchange electrons and become one. He wondered if Mr. Grenhold would know where the shelter was. In another microverse his mom would have called Spence by now and would know he wasn't staying there. In an alternate reality she was probably worried sick about him.

Heck settled into the bench. A hero didn't feel hunger, and he sure didn't complain about a toothache. A superhero didn't ask his friends to put him up for a couple of days. He roamed the streets at night without need of sleep, impervious to rain and cold. A hero didn't wait for his mom to find him. He took charge, made a plan.

He figured he'd been waiting about three hours, real time. It was getting on in the afternoon. He'd wait until he turned to bones if he had to. There wasn't anything else to do anyway.

—

He must have been in deep REM daydream, because when the landlord did come, Heck didn't see him approach until he was right in front of him. Heck made himself look reasonable, rational.

"You gonna sit here all day?" the landlord asked. His voice sounded as if his vocal cords had been burnt to a crisp. He pointed three fingers at Heck. "You gonna sit here on this bench all day like some kind of ghoul just to make me feel bad?"

"No," Heck said.

He shoved the three fingers in Heck's direction. "Don't smart-mouth me."

Just tell the truth, Heck thought. "I need my paints, Mr. Grenhold. That's all I want, and my portfolio. I need it for school. It's got all my semester work in it." He pulled out the other twenty. It trembled like a leaf in his hand. "This is all I have—for the portfolio, and the paints. And maybe my good brushes." I'll even wash your refrigerator magnets for you, he thought but refrained from saying.

Mr. Grenhold snatched the twenty out of his hand. "I'll take that toward rent owed. It's not my fault you've got a lazy, irresponsible mother who doesn't pay the rent. Just stay away. I got a paying tenant asking questions about you sitting here."

"She paid the rent. She was just late."

"Late eight months in a row makes her three months in breach of contract. Where's your father? Isn't anybody married anymore? In my day we had a word for women who had kids without a husband."

Heck stood up. He swallowed, but the spit wouldn't go down. It was sealing his throat shut. "Okay, we owe you money, but I'd appreciate it if you didn't talk about my mom like that."

The landlord took a step closer to him. "I'll talk about her all right. Who's going to stop me?"

I, Heck Superhero, avenger of single moms everywhere, will stop you!

Heck swallowed the words.

The landlord grinned.

Heck turned and walked away.

The landlord called after him, "If your mother left when I gave her notice, I wouldn't have had to get civil enforcement to change the locks. Bunch o' junk in there anyway."

As Heck walked to the mall, he thought about every possible plan.

One of his plans was to call his father.

This plan had a flaw. He had no idea where his father lived. All he knew about his father was his name. Once his mom had sketched his father's face. "That's your father," she said casually.

His mom was good at drawing. She taught him how as soon as he could hold a pencil. Heck had stared at the picture a long time, trying to see beyond the edges of the page, turning the paper to try and see his profile. For a long time Heck begged for other information, but his mom wouldn't say anything more. Finally, when he put up a big bawl, she said, "Honey, it's like this: talking about your father, it's living in the past. If I get to live in the past for anything good, then I have to live in it for the bad, too. I learned a long time ago I had to live in today if I was going to be happy, and today that's all there is of your father."

She could only be now. She couldn't imagine the future or remember the past. She was his mom now or not at all. His mom could only be here now, or not.

That was better than his dad, who was just the "not" part. His father would forever be an image on paper: flat dad, flat line. Genetic. Flat meant squashed, slottable, stackable, and if you turned sideways people didn't see you anymore. Flat meant you could sit on a bench for hours and not get your paints back.

What was he doing wrong?

Why wasn't it working?

Hadn't he given popcorn to the poor? Hadn't he folded laundry for the tired and dirty? Hadn't he played with the deeply neurotic?

He thought of the twenties that Mr. Grenhold had taken for rent. One of those really belonged to Spence.

Was that it? The stolen twenty? That probably canceled everything out. That explained why everything was going wrong: Spence's stolen twenty—which he had just now given away for the second time.

He had to come up with the Ultimate Good Deed, something that made up for an ultimate bad deed. The Good Deed was the Theory of Everything.

He could choose not to believe. If he chose evil he would have to step out of his own microverse and into an evil one. By doing that, he would condemn himself to the bottomworld, of course, but the bottomworld had super beings, too—evil nemeses of the topworld. He could be the best of the worst, the top of the bottom, the most powerful of the powerless. There was a certain logic in this course: abandoned kid becomes thief, drug user. It all went together in a way.

Or.

The Theory of Everything.

Heck walked, lost in thought, not really knowing where he was going. Even his thoughts weren't going anywhere. He couldn't think without drawing. He picked an only slightly crumpled piece of paper out of a nearby trash can, whipped out his sketching pencil, and began drawing a superhero.

Portfolio due Friday.

Today was ... Wednesday.

Self-portrait, due yesterday.

Heck drew his best superhero in a kneeling pose, his huge iron knuckles crushed against his broad, intelligent forehead, twenty-three chromosomes human, twenty-three chromosomes god.

Mr. B. would rap his knuckles for drawing superheroes. Avoidance behavior, he'd say. He drew a word bubble for the superhero and wrote in it: "And what of this kindly fanboy artist who stood between his mother and destruction ..."

Heck crumpled the drawing. Maybe she'd called. Maybe Spence knew where she was by now.

He had to call Spence. Good thing he hadn't used all his change for a chocolate bar.

Spence's mom picked up the phone. Heck hung up.

A few minutes later he dialed again. This time Spence picked it up. "Hi, Heck."

"How did you know it was me?" Heck asked.

"Mom recognized your breathing. She wants to know if you're okay."

"She can tell something is wrong by my breathing?"

"Well, you haven't been here in a couple of days, and then you hang up on her. She wonders if you're mad at her or something."

That was how she got to know you, Spence's mom, by asking if everything was okay. The FBI should turn over their most tight-lipped cases to her. She'd have them blubbering their whole lives in minutes.

"I'm not mad at her," Heck said. "Tell her everything's okay."

Spence lowered his voice. That was a good sign. It meant hypertime was still their secret. "Look, I'm sorry I hung up on you last time, Heck. What I really wanted to say was, you should come here and stay. Please."

"No."

"Just one night."

"Your mom would be able to tell something was wrong.

She has this psychic ability."

Dead air hung between them for a moment. Heck was afraid to ask the question. Spence was afraid to answer.

"Heck, your mom hasn't called," Spence said at last. More dead air. "You have to come live with me, Heck. I'll tell my parents your house flooded or something."

"We live—lived—on the third floor," Heck said.

"I'll tell them something."

"I almost had a job in an art gallery, sort of an entry-level position."

"So, if you just keep missing school and sleeping in a car and doing Good Deeds, your mom's going to show up with an apartment and no one will get into trouble?"

"Yes. No. I mean—"

Spence made a drippingly scornful sound that was a cross between a snort and a laugh. "You are making no sense. You have to come here, or tell someone and get some help."

"You don't understand about the kind of help they give you," Heck said. "If they get to help you, they get to punish you, too. You just don't know. I have to figure out what I did wrong and reverse it."

"You didn't do anything wrong, Heck. Well, maybe Velocity Nine."

"And the twenty," Heck said.

"What?"

"The twenty—that I borrowed."

"Twenty ... ?"

"Okay, okay, I stole it. But I'll pay it back. I promise." Heck felt a hundred percent better already. "I'm sorry."

"No one even noticed," Spence said glumly. Heck could tell he was mad about having to be nice about this when he was already mad about something else. "I'll cancel the debt if you'll come and stay here tonight."

"Thanks."

"No thanks needed. Just come."

"Listen, Spence, I want to try one more thing first. If it doesn't work out, then ... but it will. Can you look something up for me? I need to know where the shelter is. I'm thinking maybe Mom made her way there. Can you look in the phone-book under, I don't know, 'Shelters,' I guess."

He could hear Spence flip through the phonebook. "Sharpening Service, Sheet Metal Work, Shelving ... No, nothing under Shelters."

"Try Social Services."

"Okay, there's something here called the Women's Drop-In Center. It's on the corner of 26th and McLeod. So are you coming to school tomorrow? If you don't, Mr. Bandras is going to blow a blood vessel. He's asking questions."

"Yeah, I know. I'll—I'll go."

"Tomorrow?"

"I've missed so much," Heck said, sighing. "A math test and a social studies presentation that I know of. Everyone will be on my case."

"Yeah, well, stay away longer, then. That should fix everything." All the fight had gone out of Spence's voice.

"All my books and notes and stuff are gone. Mr. Grenhold

had everything hauled away."

"Good reason to flush your life," Spence said.

Heck could feel his teeth vibrating at high frequency. He didn't know why he didn't attract every dog in town. "Okay. Well, I'm going to hang up now," he said.

"Don't hang up, Heck! Tell me where you are."

"I can't. You'll tell."

"Freaking right I'll tell!" Spence stopped, took a deep breath, and said, "Look, Heck, I think I understand. If you tell ... If people find out and your mom gets in trouble, then you won't be her hero anymore."

Heck nodded, forgetting that he was on the phone.

"But maybe if we just tried to explain ..."

"Topworld people don't understand bottomworld language," Heck said. "Mutant–human relations have never been good."

He thought, just before he hung up, that he could hear Spence practicing his swearing.

When he opened the phone booth, Marion stood there. Heck screamed.

"What are you doing here?" he asked when he got his breath again.

"The pocket creatures told me to watch out for you. I know what it feels like to have no friends," Marion said.

"Then you met the pocket creatures and they've been your friends ever since." Heck started walking and Marion trailed behind him. He stopped. "Marion, why are you following me?"

"When you do your superhero thing, I want to be there to see it."

"Look, I'm not a superhero, I told you."

"What's your mission tonight?"

Heck shoved his hands into his pockets. "I have to go to the Drop-In Center, corner of 26th and McLeod."

"Do you know where that is?"

"No."

"I do," Marion said, beaming. "I'll take you there."

Heck sighed, and followed Marion.

"How did you find out you were a superhero, anyway?" Marion asked.

"I told you, I'm not really a—" He stopped. It was hopeless. "Okay. Okay, I'll tell you, Marion. This is the absolute truth: a social worker told me I was a superkid."

Marion's eyes were on high beam. "Wow."

"And before that, my mom always called me her hero." Two true things.

"Are you the only one? Are there others?"

"Lots," Heck said. He couldn't stop himself now. "There are superheroes all over the place. They just lay low about it, but it usually comes out anyway. Like Mother Teresa. Tried to hide herself in a convent and look what happened. Some cash in on it, like Michael Jordan. They just make sure they don't, you know, overdo it. There might be questions. Tiger Woods, the same—loses a game every so often so there won't be any suspicions."

Marion was nodding like a bobble-head toy.

He just wanted to play.

Heck wanted to play, too. He could see right before his eyes what could happen to you if you played so hard and long you ceased to interface with microversal reality. But Heck was pretty hungry in this reality. Marion was just a kid, older than Heck, but younger, too. He felt bad for how he'd treated him.

"So, Marion, uh, tell me about these pet aliens of yours," Heck said. "How big do they get?"

"They're fully grown, but most naked eyes can't see them. They came here on an asteroid that swings by sometimes, but they belong on the fifth planet. The one they think isn't there anymore." He looked down protectively at his jacket. "On May 5 I'll have to give them back."

"How old are you, Marion?"

"Seven thousand four hundred and three," he said.

"What's that in earth years?"

"Eighteen."

They walked in silence. Heck kicked a small piece of broken cement, and then Marion kicked it, and then Heck. They took turns like that for three blocks until the cement fell into a sewer grating.

"The pocket creatures trust you," Marion said. "They really want you to help them return to their planet."

"And how do you do that?"

"I have to release them."

"Release them?"

"They have to be released at just the right time from a

certain height and on a certain trajectory." Marion was looking at him with those high-beam eyes. Heck wondered if this guy had x-ray vision. He wasn't looking at him as much as through him. He wondered if Marion could see his stomach folded up like an empty wallet.

"Marion, where do you live?"

"Here," Marion said, and shrugged.

"How do you survive? What do you eat?"

"There's places. I'll show you. But I'm usually not hungry."

"How do you get that big without being hungry?"

"I know I'm fat."

"I didn't say ... You aren't fat, but you are big."

Marion stood looking at him with a strange dignity. "So, will you help me?"

"Sure. I'll help you." Heck couldn't believe he'd just said that. Maybe his reality-effacing self had escaped completely into a parallel world.

Marion smiled, a full-blown, all-dimple smile. When he blinked it was like the headlights were flashing. He picked up Heck's hand as if it were something he'd dropped. He held it with his two hands, studying it. Heck hoped he wasn't going to kiss it or something.

"It's still attached," Heck said. "To me."

Marion didn't let go, so Heck snatched it away.

Marion blinked at the spot where Heck's hand had been. "I heard you talking on the phone. I'm not sure where my mom is, either. She died when I was little."

Heck had thought being dead gave you a fairly permanent address. "Sorry," he said.

Marion stopped talking, and Heck couldn't think of anything to say, so they walked in silence. They came to 26th, and walked a few blocks along it until they were at McLeod. The shelter was an old yellow house with a verandah. "That's it," Marion said.

Being so close to his mom now made Heck feel even sorrier for Marion. "If you were little you probably don't remember your mother much," he said.

Marion shook his head at the sidewalk. After a minute he said, "I remember one thing. I came home one day and my pockets were full of stuff, and I wanted to show her. I remember that. She knelt down on the floor and looked at everything I'd found. I think there was an exploded pen and a Scratch n' Win card or something. They weren't anything much, but she acted like I'd found treasure."

Heck wasn't thinking about how to get away from Marion anymore. "You must miss her a lot," he said.

Marion shrugged. "That's all I remember about her. Her hands, and her voice. I don't remember her face, really." He turned away. "I don't feel like playing anymore," he said. He walked away, his back straight. He didn't even talk to his pockets.

Heck watched him for a minute.

There were two kinds of being gone. There was hypertime gone and there was dead gone, and Heck felt lucky that his mom was only the former.

—

He entered the shelter. A woman with white hair smiled at him. "This shelter is for women only, honey."

"I'm looking for my mom, Estelle. Estelle Berlioz."

Heck waited while she checked some papers on her desk.

"I'm sorry, young man, but I don't have anyone here by the name of Berlioz."

"She might be confused," Heck said. "If I could go in ..."

"I'm sorry, no men allowed, not even small ones. We can't have the public coming in and gawking at our guests."

"But ..."

"What does she look like?" the woman asked.

"Well, she's small, not much taller than me, and built slight, and she has straight hair, blond, and she has a tattoo on her shoulder—an old-fashioned tricycle."

"Sorry, hon. I'm sure we don't have anyone here who fits that description."

"But ..."

"Honest."

Heck stared at her, mouth open.

"Do you want me to phone someone for you, young man?"

"No. No, thanks," he said quietly.

He left, feeling like he was wading through quantum foam, like waist-high styrofoam balls. Where?

She must have gone to that guy's house. What was his name? Sam. Sam Halstead. She went there to get her check, of course.

Maybe she stayed, on condition that he didn't get too serious. What was the address? Near Lindsay Park, Levi had told him. He headed in that direction, calling upon his superpowers of memory to click with an address before he got there.

She would have to be way far into hypertime to stay gone this long or to seek refuge at Sam's.

Hypertime. The bridge to coexisting realities. There was the reality that included her son Heck, but that reality included heartless landlords and no place to live. She couldn't live there.

It was possible she was going to construct a reality with this Sam of ... Morrow Drive, that was it. Maybe that was why she hadn't called. Maybe she was going to a reality in which she had no son to interfere in a new relationship.

It made Heck sad to think of that, but it would also be comforting to know she was all right, and that someone was taking care of her. His big fear, the one that made him want to throw up to think of it, was that she was headed into the dimension of not existing at all. He didn't know how he knew it, but he'd known for a long time that she'd thought about that dimension. A lot.

He had to find her and tell her: Mom, choose any reality you want, as long as it's not that one. If it makes you happy, choose Sam of 356 ... 356! Morrow Drive.

It was a box house, with box windows, all dark, and a box stoop. All it needed was a big satin ribbon to be the best present Heck ever got. He didn't know what time it was for the first time in his life. It was an unsettling feeling, like he'd just lost track of the spin of the earth. This was how his mom felt all the time, he thought. It must be, for her, like trying to jump onto a spinning merry-go-round.

Heck hesitated before ringing the bell. It was late. Or maybe really early. Other people's houses were dark, too. Then he remembered that it wouldn't matter to his mom if it was late. She didn't care about things like that. She'd be glad to see him. She was probably just at that very moment having bad dreams about missing her son, her hero.

He rang the bell.

His mom had never figured this world out. Just like he had never figured out radicals in math. He'd tried and tried, but he just didn't get it. His mom just didn't get it. It wasn't her fault. He didn't know how she'd been getting by without him. Who was keeping her running grocery list?

Heck knocked on the door.

Radicals. Ha! Radicals didn't seem so bad anymore. In fact, the whole idea of school sounded good. He'd be glad to get back. Lovely bell telling you what to do, where to go, user-friendly teachers ...

Heck rang the doorbell again, and knocked as hard as he could. Then he thought he saw the curtain move, so slightly it was possible he could have imagined it.

"Mom?" he said toward the window.

He waited. Maybe she was coming to the door. Maybe she was worried that he was a dread interloper.

He put his mouth up against the crack of the door. "Mom?" he whispered. "It's Heck."

Could he hear her breathing on the other side of the door?

"Mom, if you can hear me ..."

He listened. He couldn't hear anything now, but he thought he could feel her there.

"Mom ... Mom ... I just wanted you to know that everything's okay. I mean, don't worry about anything ... Spence's house is great ... Hey, I hope this new boyfriend is treating you nice. I met this kid named Marion—who'd name their son Marion, eh? You'd never guess what he has in his pockets. Aliens! Germ-sized aliens ... Ha ha ... I think he's just playing, just got playing and couldn't quit ... So, um ..."

Heck pressed up against the door as if it were his mom. He leaned into it, put his lips near the doorjamb.

"Speaking of Marion, I figured something out, Mom, when I was walking here. You know it's not really safe on a bridge between two dimensions. Take me, for example. One of me is real, and one of me is where I dream, you know? I guess I have to get the pieces together, or I'll be ... split. Never Superman and never Clark Kent. I won't be able to fly, but I won't be able to walk like everyone else either. I'll always be standing in this phone booth with nothing to change into and nothing to change out of, just standing there in my underwear ..." Heck chuckled. His mom would like that one. "So, well anyway, Mom, do what you have to do, you know? Just be happy, and then I'll be okay."

Just then a car pulled up in front of the house. A man got out—the one his mom had dated. Sam. He stood by his car facing Heck.

"Is there a problem, son?" He began walking slowly toward Heck. "You're Estelle's boy," he said.

Heck nodded. He glanced at the window. The curtains were still. He swallowed. "I—I thought maybe she was staying here," he said. Sam wasn't a bad-looking guy, but he wasn't nearly good enough for his mom. "Have you seen her? Levi said he was told to forward her check to this address."

Sam stopped at the bottom of the stoop and rubbed the back of his neck. "Yes, she showed up yesterday."

"Did she say anything?"

"She asked for her check, but it isn't here yet."

"That's it? She didn't say where she was going or anything?"

The man shook his head. After considering a moment he said, "She did say something else, but I didn't really understand her. It sounded like—like the same conversation we had a month ago, like she was back at that day, telling me she couldn't go out with me."

She was out of real time altogether, now. Keep it light, he told himself.

"Guess she didn't like you, huh?"

"We had a good time," the man said, "but she's busy with her first love." Heck held his breath. "That would be you, son. She told me to call her in a couple of years when you were older."

Don't think, Heck told himself. Don't think. Not yet. Just nod—mature, sane nod. "Well, if you see her, can you tell her everything's okay?"

THURSDAY, MAY 5

His stomach shrunk up into a crampy ball and his teeth screamed into his ear. It hurt to swallow.

This was bad. Bad, bad, bad. His mom was so far into hypertime she was having a time warp. She was lost. What if she didn't really belong to this microverse? What if she was mutant maladaptive and was never meant to exist here at all?

What if she was?

When the world was tipped over and everything that normally held you down like apartments and portfolios was shaking off into space, you had to grab on to something. He wasn't going to let go of his mom.

He had to find her. He was going to have to go to the police, talk to Mr. Holland, get them to put out an all-points bulletin, tell them about his teeth.

No. Not his teeth. If they found her, she'd be sad all over again if they knew about his teeth. Besides, if you were a superhero, you laughed at pain—especially toothache pain. Ha ha! He submitted to the pain. He let it wash over him, studied it, observed it like it was happening to some distant part of him instead of in the core of his brain. A miracle.

He passed the Art Store. Stopped.

Closed. Dark.

Heck pressed his face up against the glass. It felt cool, the way his mom's hand felt when she touched his face.

Going to the police would be the end of their secret that Everything Wasn't Necessarily Okay. If he went to the police, they would find her, but maybe nothing would be the same again. Would they put him in a frosty home? Think. There had to be another way.

There was still the Good Deed.

Spence would snort and swear, but Heck believed.

Maybe he just needed a really Big Good Deed, an Ultimate Good Deed, one that could find mothers in hypertime. He thought about every Good Deed he could do with no money and no house and no résumé. He could let the animals out of the zoo, or stand in front of an oncoming truck and have his organs donated. No. Someone would shoot at the animals, and no one had a use for flattened eyeballs. He pressed his lips against the glass, then his other cheek. His teeth were crying, and then he was.

He stepped back, rubbed his face with his left sleeve, rubbed the window with his right sleeve.

He had to go to the police.

No, their whole life would be busted.

Yes. He had to. He was sick, and his mom was ... who knew where she was, what was happening to her?

No. If he told, maybe having no apartment would be the least of her problems.

But yes, because what was the big deal about a frosty home if his mom was dead?

He shuddered just thinking the word. Yes, he had to go to the police.

No. If he told the police, that might be what killed her.

Yes.

No.

Yes.

Heck stepped back from the window so he wouldn't break it if he felt an irresistible urge to start smashing his head repeatedly against something hard.

He needed to draw. He needed to play. Where was Marion?

He needed the Good Deed. He needed it bad right now, even if it was just to make himself feel better. He put his hands around his eyes and peered into the Art Store. Maybe he could get in through the broken window and clean up again, free this time. That would be a Good Deed. Maybe it would be all right if he took some paper to draw some superheroes.

A new painting had been put in the window. It was of a young girl happily cutting out paper dolls from a newspaper, but as she cut, the paper bled. The dolls writhed in agony.

Heck stared. Even his teeth weren't louder than that.

He'd always known paintings could make things happen. This painting made you want to punch something or go home and sit in the car while it ran for a long time in an enclosed space. You had to be good to do a painting like that. You had to be willing to follow your nightmares around and take tweezers to the waste products of your brain. But what if you could make a painting that made you want to share your oatmeal and bring flowers to your gramma's grave? Instead of painting what was ugly in the world, what if you painted what was beautiful? Wouldn't that be a Good Deed? What if you showed the world something beautiful where no one had seen beautiful before? Like Marion—everyone treated him like mutant maladaptive, but they didn't see that light in his eyes, didn't see how good he was at playing.

What if a painting could be the ultimate Good Deed? What if it could change the world? Or even the entire microverse of one person?

He would paint Marion.

He felt strange, as if he'd stepped over some invisible line and there was no going back. He was Superkid, capable of making peanut butter cookies and signing permission forms in a single bound. He was Superkid, in charge of popcorn for the poor and self-esteem for the downtrodden. He felt better already.

He'd been walking a long time, but he didn't hurt. The Theory of Everything Is Going to Be Okay was written in a bubble, in script, flowing and exquisitely thin. It was all poetry.

Heck knew that even if he stood still Marion would find him eventually. Looking for him didn't take long.

"Where have you been?" Marion asked. "I've been looking all over for you."

"I've been looking for you, too, Marion." Heck's eyes fastened on him.

Why hadn't he seen it before? Here the Good Deed had been in front of his eyes all along and he hadn't known it. He would introduce Marion to Marion through the Good Deed of the painting.

"Thanks, Marion," Heck said, putting his hand on Marion's shoulder. "Thanks for helping me be a superhero."

For a moment Marion was silent. Then he said, "It's Thursday, Heck. May 5."

"May 5," Heck said happily. "I've never known you to lie to me."

"Today is the day," Marion said.

"Yes, it is. The day for what?"

"You know—the Good Deed," Marion said.

Once in a while in the world, didn't everything fall into place? Once in a while, didn't the whole world make sense?

"Just what I was thinking," Heck said.

They stood looking at each other. Marion was hugging his jacket tightly to himself.

"Well," Heck said gently. "Well, it's May 5."

"The day the spores have to be released," Marion said. "Did you forget? It has to be today."

"It's humanity I want to save, not aliens," Heck said, smiling. "But ... sure."

Marion nodded and whispered something comforting to

the inside pockets of his jacket. Heck thought, why didn't they let him sleep with a coat on? What was so bad about inventing friends if you didn't have any of the real kind? There he was, shifting from foot to foot as if he had to go to the bathroom.

Heck said, "But Marion, before that I'm going to paint you."

"Paint me?"

"That's right," Heck said. "I know where we can get some paints."

"No."

"No? Why not?"

"I—I get this dream. I'm scared of being painted."

Heck took Marion's elbow. "Come on, old phobe, we're going to the Art Store. It's the Good Deed. It's the one. You're going to see how beautiful you are."

"The Art Store? It's not open."

"It's okay. I've got it worked out."

Marion followed silently. After a minute he said in a low voiced, "I'm scared. If we get caught ..."

"We won't get caught," Heck said cheerfully.

Marion was quiet as they walked to the Art Store. He didn't clutch at his coat or talk to his pockets all the way there. He just walked close beside Heck.

Heck looked up at the sky. When did he know the cosmos was so beautiful? When he was eight and he found out the galaxy swirled like the little windmill his mom had bought him at the circus? Maybe it happened the day he understood that atoms looked like the solar system. Just knowing that made him happy, made the microverse make sense. He wondered if tiny beings lived on electrons and woke up each day to a nucleus sun. Probably his own solar system was an atom in God's body. Anything could happen in a cosmos that was part math and part magic.

When they arrived at the Art Store, the first thing Heck did was clean up the back alley area.

"Why?" Marion asked.

"We have to earn the paint," Heck said.

"If we get caught, they won't care that we cleaned up for them," Marion said morosely.

"Don't worry, Marion. I'll pay him back, in cash too, once I get some."

"Are you sure?"

"Would a superhero do anything else?"

Marion started helping.

"Besides," Heck said, "I know the owner. I don't think he cares about those paints."

Heck worked faster than Marion, but Marion picked up the heavy stuff: a box of rained-on paper, some discarded pipe.

"There. I think that's worth a canvas," Heck said after a while. He slipped a finger into the warped window and found the broken latch, and a moment later they both eased in.

Marion was vibrating. "Can we hurry?"

"You can't hurry art," Heck said, rummaging in the dusty art supplies. He was in the zone, he already knew his painting, the heart of it.

It was like entering the Speed Force to play with those paints. Heck felt FVF, fine very fine. He knew he wanted his painting to reflect the fact that quarks came in three colors—red, green, and blue. He glanced at Marion weaving among the paintings, and remembered that they came in six flavors, too. His favorites were Up, Down, Strange, and Charm.

Heck mixed quark paints. A moment later he was NM, near mint. His teeth felt tiny in his mouth, whimpering quietly.

Marion wandered among the displays of artwork while Heck found the paints and a palette and a canvas. As he mixed the colors, he could hear Marion talking to the spores. Heck set up the easel just as Marion emerged from between two paintings as if through an interdimensional portal.

"Just stand there like that," Heck said. "That's good."

At first Marion looked pained and afraid. "It's getting lighter out," he said.

"It's still dark."

"But not *as* dark. I'm tired."

Heck got him a chair.

He fidgeted and Heck had to remind him several times to sit still.

"What time does the owner come?" Marion asked.

"It's all right," Heck said. "We'll be gone long before he comes."

Heck remembered simplicity. There was nothing simpler than space strings falling like ribbons and confetti, nothing simpler than seeing the real essence of Marion Ewald burn through the membranes of higher dimensions. Heck didn't forget he was painting Marion in the hopes of finding a small mother in a big city, but it became good for its own self. He was uber-painter, he was the maker of the perfect Good Deed. Maybe it was changing the world even now, curing the sewer-dwellers driven to evil by grief, feeding Froot Loops to the flesh-eaters ... It was as if a hundred hands from every part of the multiverse were helping him, and he was pretty sure he was experiencing the Theory of Everything.

Marion nodded off for a while, and Heck painted from memory. When Marion woke up, he leapt out of the chair.

"It's morning!"

"I know," Heck said. He was sweating, exhausted, but he felt good. "I'm almost done."

"Almost? We have to go! Someone's going to be here ..."

"Okay, okay. It's done."

Heck signed his name and set the painting among the others. He gazed at it. In it, Marion was both a particle and a wave, bending space and time. Reality had responded to the artist's touch. Everyone in the world was art if you just looked at him hard and long enough.

"Is that me?" Marion asked.

"That's you," Heck said.

"That's not me. That guy's not fat."

"That's you," Heck said.

"But I'm not ugly in this picture."

"You're not ugly," Heck said, gazing at the picture with pleasure. It said all the secret good things about Marion, and all the sad things, and something beyond sad, something that Heck couldn't name.

Marion peered at the painting, got closer, moved to one side and then the other.

"I look ... nice."

"You are nice."

"How do you make that light come out of my eyes?"

"Yeah," Heck said, "how *do* you?"

Marion stroked his pockets. He seemed to have forgotten about people coming to open the gallery.

Heck studied his face. "How do you feel, Marion, now that you can see the way you really are?"

"It's good, but ..."

Heck held his breath, waiting for the whole world to change for Marion.

Marion shrugged. He said again, "It's good, but ..."

Why wasn't it working?

Marion said, "It's May 5. I have to release the spores."

Heck's heart went flat as a valentine. What did the spores have to do with it? "But you're supposed to see ... Can't you see your quantum self, how unique you are?"

Marion looked at the eyes in the painting. Heck saw that he'd painted them too bright. No. They'd been that bright before, but they weren't that bright now, like the battery had run down on them.

"I'm hungry," Marion said. "Let's eat first."

"But you're never—! All right. Let's get out of here."

"Don't leave me. It's May 5."

"I won't leave you," Heck said.

On the way to the mall, Heck figured out the Very Important Thing.

All the Good Deeds he'd done so far had been about him. The lost little girl had been about possible doughnuts. Being nice to Marion had been about getting rid of him, at least at first. Painting him had been about finding his mom.

But he knew now. A Good Deed had power only if you did it for someone else. Pure. No hopes attached. No reward in mind. That was where he'd gone wrong. He couldn't think of a time he'd done that—the pure Good Deed, something completely unselfish, something that proved true supergoodness.

The painting came close. He could feel it. Something was going to come out of that painting. It hadn't done what he'd hoped. It hadn't made Marion want to live in the same microverse as everyone else. But Marion was hungry. That had to be something. And the painting ... Well, it was beautiful.

Once at the mall, Heck sat on a bench. "You go ahead, Marion," he said. "I need to sit for a bit."

"I'll get you a burger," Marion said.

"No. No, thanks."

What would he do now about his mom?

"I have money."

"I made a vow. I don't take money from my friends anymore," Heck said. He was out of ideas. He'd just have to go to the police and bust the whole family.

"Well, welcome to the land of answered prayers," someone said behind him.

Heck leapt to his feet. "Spence!"

Heck stared and Spence grinned and Marion just stood nearby like a big navy blue cloud.

"Look at you. You're dirty," Spence said.

"Maybe I'm just not fashion-conscious," Heck said, smiling.

"Maybe you're just not conscious, period," Spence said.

They both laughed and knocked knuckles.

"So," Heck said.

"Yeah ... so ..." Spence held out a small white pill.

"Thanks," Heck said. "Just one?"

"Shove it right into the hole in your tooth and hold it there. That's right. As it dissolves, pack it firmly into the hole."

The bitterness of the aspirin filled the back of Heck's throat, but in seconds his teeth felt better.

"Ahh. Thank you." He sat down. In a minute he asked, "How did you know I was here?"

"Cosmic awareness," Spence said.

"Serious," Heck said. "How did you know?"

"I am serious. Cosmic awareness is a guide to wherever you are needed most, remember?" He shrugged and leaned back. "Yesterday I went to Mr. Hill's T-Bird, but it was gone. Then this morning I remembered you came here to wait for your mom when you lost your key once." He crossed his arms and shoved his hands into his armpits. He looked at Marion and shifted uncomfortably.

"This is Marion Ewald, my friend," Heck said.

Spence said a weak hello, and Marion nodded. Heck's teeth had gone to sleep.

They were silent for a while. Then Heck said, "She hasn't called yet, has she."

Spence shook his head. "Heck, what if she never calls?" The superhero strained his huge shoulders and managed a small shrug.

Spence imitated him and shrugged too. "What? What does that mean?" He shrugged again. "Does it mean yes I don't know anything take me home and take care of me? Cause that's what I think you should do, Heck. Just come to my place for a few days."

Marion nodded.

"Your hair is greasy and you've got these shadows under your eyes ... Splashpage, Heck. Atomic radiation might turn comic book people into superheroes, but in real life it just turns you into a shadow on the wall."

Marion nodded at everything Spence said, as if he could bring about world peace by agreeing with everyone.

"You're right," Heck said.

"And besides that, you—what did you say?"

"I've tried everything, Spence, but I just can't find her. I've got to tell ... somebody, I guess. But I have this guy to think about." He inclined his head toward Marion, who was stroking his pockets and looking worried.

"This guy needs help," Spence said.

"I've been taking care of him," Heck said.

"Heck, you can't take care of a goldfish," Spence said.

That was low, Heck thought. He should never have told Spence about his goldfish.

Spence sighed. "Look, maybe both of you can come to my house."

Heck looked at Marion. The dimples from his cheeks had teleported to his forehead. He was going to cry this time for sure.

"It's May 5," Marion said weakly.

Heck said, "I promised him I'd help him release the spores."

"Spores?"

"It's kind of hard to explain. I promised," Heck said.

"I'm afraid you won't come," Spence said.

"I'll come. I just can't leave Marion."

"He might never come."

Heck wanted to explain about Marion, about how you could play and play until playing was all there was.

Spence swore. "None of this would have happened if your mom—" He stopped.

Heck looked into Spence's eyes, trying to find a way to answer.

That was when their molecular joining clicked in. Right at that moment. Heck knew Spence was seeing deep down to his DNA. Heck made him remember all about his mom and how she was with watches. He made Spence remember that every Halloween she told them scary stories in the graveyard until they screamed at the slightest sound and had to sleep with the lights on. He knew Spence remembered that she sometimes didn't come home at night, but he also made him remember how she broke up with a boyfriend because he said he didn't like Heck's artwork all over the house.

He made Spence remember second grade. He came to school without a lunch, and when the teacher asked why, Heck told her, "We don't have any food." The next day a social worker showed up, asking lots of questions, reminding his mom about the frosty home time, hinting that they could take Heck away from her.

He made Spence remember how much she suffered in hypertime.

"Heck, I ..."

It worked every time.

"I promised Mr. Bandras I'd bring you home ..."

The molecular joining stopped.

Heck felt himself swelling up like the Incredible Hulk. "You told Mr. Bandras?"

Spence's I'm sorry face was gone. "Heck ..."

"You told Mr. Bandras!"

"He's spent so much time with you in art class. I thought ... Remember he gave you that old portfolio of his that wasn't even old? He likes you. Heck, he knew something was wrong anyway. He went to your apartment yesterday when you didn't show up at school. I had to tell him something."

Heck felt like he did when they played Hangman. When he won he always drew blood dripping out of the eyes and mouth of the stick man. He drew lolling tongues and twitching arms.

When Spence won, he just left the stick man as it was, a blind, speechless hole. Heck sat there with stick arms and stick legs and a coin-round head and no mouth at all. He said, "You'd better go."

Spence went.

Heck had the feeling he'd just lost the game.

He looked at Marion. Marion looked back. Blink. Blink.

What was he doing? Spence was right. He couldn't take care of Marion, or his mom, or even himself for that matter. What was wrong with him? He had to run after Spence right now and say, "I'm sorry. You're right. I'll talk to your mom."

He stood up. Marion looked at him. Blink. Blink.

"Marion, come with me to Spence's."

Marion frowned. "It's May 5."

"Look, I've got a place to go, but I want you to come too."

Marion's head hung. "The pocket lint is almost gone."

"Marion, if I help you release the spores, then will you come with me?"

He had a sneaky look on his face. "It's May 5," he repeated stubbornly.

"All right. All right. Let's go, then," Heck said.

It was dark by the time they arrived at a street lamp across the street from the parking garage.

"Is this it?" Heck asked.

Marion didn't move. "I think I hear something," he whispered. "Cyborgs."

Heck listened. There was nothing but traffic noise. "Come on."

Maybe the painting hadn't changed the microverse for Marion, but it had changed it for Heck. He felt good, even though his teeth were screaming again and he could hear the fizzy popping sounds in his jaw and it hurt to talk. He felt good, even though Marion kept saying, "It's going to be okay, right, Heck? Is it going to be okay?" and Heck kept answering, "Everything's okay."

He was glad he was going to Spence's. He'd just figured out that sometimes telling was like looking. It was what you had to do before you could change reality. That was what Mr. B. had been trying to tell him about drawing superheroes. Quantum theory said you could alter reality, but you had to acknowledge the one you were in first.

"How do you know?"

"Huh?"

"How do you know everything's going to be okay?"

Heck opened his mouth, then shut it again. Finally he said, "Okay, maybe not everything. But Spence's mom is nice. She'll make us talk, but she'll stick up for us."

"I can't."

"You can't what? Release the spores? Okay, we'll try again next May 5."

"No!" Marion said sadly. "No, it has to be today."

They entered the parking garage and started up the stairs. On the third floor they stopped.

Marion looked around anxiously. "One more," he said.

"No, this is it," Heck said.

"All right. Over there," Marion said. Together they approached the waist-high cement wall. "I'll release them from there."

"Then we'll go to Spence's house and his mom will peel us some kiwis ..."

"No."

"Yes."

Marion shook his head.

Heck looked into Marion's eyes, looked hard into them. What was it he wanted? To be sure he'd be safe? Maybe it was to know if Heck believed in the pocket creatures. But he'd given Marion everything he could on that.

No. That wasn't it.

Marion didn't need anyone else to believe. If it started out as a game, like when Heck played at being a superhero, it wasn't a game anymore. It was the dimension Marion lived in now. He'd played until he couldn't stop.

What, then? Heck wanted to ask, looking into Marion's eyes. What did he need?

Then he knew.

Marion needed Heck to do a Good Deed that was less about saving him and more about being his friend. Heck knew, now that he'd painted him, that he could be that for him.

"Marion, have you ever heard of molecular joining?" Heck asked him.

Marion shook his head.

"Well, it's what only the best of friends can do. I've done it with my best friend, Spence."

"No, thanks." Marion wrapped his coat tightly around himself. "I don't like boys that way."

"It's going to be okay, Marion. Come on. Just relax and look at me. Look in my eyes."

Heck looked into Marion's eyes. The pupils dilated easily. In a few moments he was past the cornea, through the pupil, and floating in vitreous fluid toward the retina.

Marion sucked his breath in, but he didn't move.

The trick was not letting anything like dimples or pocket creatures throw you off. Optic nerve, rods and cones, horizontal and bipolar and amacrine cells to the axons of the ganglion cells ... Heck didn't really know what it was to fly, but he thought it might feel like this.

"What are you doing to me?" Marion whimpered, but his eyes widened and that only helped.

"Shhh. It's okay. It's the molecular joining."

Marion gripped his coat around himself, but his eyes didn't move away. He didn't even blink.

Heck was in.

At first, swimming in Marion's brain was like reading a Johnny Craig comic. Exploded pens and scratched-up Scratch n' Win cards and marbles and bent paper clips floated between the ganglions of his brain. Heck was free-falling in cytoplasm, entering a nucleus, climbing on ladders of DNA ...

"Now," Heck whispered.

A molecule split and Heck plugged in: adenine, thymine,

cytosine, guanine ... joining ...

It was done.

Molecular joining.

And as soon as he was plugged in, he let it happen on his end too.

Together they walked around in Marion's brain.

The dimension of Your Mother Is Dead.

It was a bleak one. Who hugged you in this dimension? Who kissed your face when it had acne and no girl your own age was going to kiss it for years or at least until you had a good car?

Who made you cocoa in this dimension? Who touched your forehead when you had a fever?

It was a dry, dusty cratered moon of a dimension, and Heck could hardly breathe in its atmosphere.

Heck imagined Marion as a six-year-old. *Let's play*, he would say to Heck.

I can't breathe here, Heck thought into the airless space.

Stay and play.

"Come out here and play," Heck said. He had to get out. There was something in Marion's brain worse than a Johnny Craig comic book, something that scared Heck.

The six-year-old looked away.

"It's okay, I'm your friend."

But that wasn't the microverse they were in now. Heck felt so sorry about that. He hugged the six-year-old, and he vanished, and Heck was hugging the big, real Marion.

He let go. He and Marion were molecularly joined.

"We're friends, right?" Heck said, and his voice said it the way his heart meant it.

Marion nodded slowly. He picked up Heck's paint-stained hand, held it in his two hands like he'd done before, like Heck's hand was something he'd found on the floor. Heck didn't pull away this time.

"Don't think you didn't do a good thing for me," Marion said quietly. He smiled, a one-dimple smile. "The best thing."

Heck's eyes stung and his throat hurt, and his teeth knew he wasn't painting anymore.

Marion's smile faded. "But it's still May 5."

He dropped Heck's hand and undid his top coat button.

"You'll see," Heck said.

"Help," Marion said, undoing another button.

"We'll get help. We'll stick together ..."

Marion undid the last button. His hands were trembling and tears were streaming down his face. He was wearing a gray T-shirt underneath his coat. There was something naked and appalling about that T-shirt.

"Hey, Marion," Heck said, putting his hand on Marion's shoulder. "I have an idea. How about if we just take the spores to Spence's house and release them from his bedroom window. Or keep them. I'm pretty sure Spence has a lot of pocket lint."

"No." Marion had his headlight eyes on, and they were crying, but then he smiled. It was the biggest thirteen-dimple smile Heck had ever seen. "Thanks. Thanks for playing with me. You'll find your mom, Heck. The spores told me so."

Heck saw it in slow motion, what happened then.

He saw it frame by frame, as Marion flung his jacket over the wall, over, gone, and in a single bound mounted the wall and jumped after it.

As if he could fly.

Heck ran down the stairs to the street below. Marion was on his back, bleeding out of his ears, and still. His eyes were open.

"Help!" Heck screamed. "Help!"

He jumped to his feet and waved his arms at a passing car. The car stopped. The driver took one look at Marion and reached for his cell phone.

Heck went back to Marion. "Pulse. Pulse," he whispered. He pressed Marion's neck, his wrist. Maybe he wasn't doing it right. Heck could hear himself making a strange "uhn, uhn" sound. He tried to stop but couldn't. The blood was draining out of his brain and filling up with negative space.

"Are you breathing?" Heck said, giving Marion a shake. "Breathe! Uhn, uhn."

He put his mouth over Marion's and breathed into it. Should have seen it coming, should have ... He breathed into Marion's mouth again. Again. Again. All the rage in Heck's lungs stormed into Marion's mouth. Again. Blink! Why don't you blink!

He could hear the steps approaching. Heck jumped up, roaring. "Help!"

It was the police.

"Help," Heck gulped. "He fell—from up there ..." His heart was ticking like a bomb. It was going to explode if Marion didn't blink those headlight eyes.

One of the officers knelt down while the other radioed someone.

"What happened here?"

"He fell ..." Heck breathed into his mouth again, forced air into him.

"What's his name?"

Breathe. "Marion."

"That's a girl's name."

Heck started to cry. The "uhn, uhn" sound turned into big, ugly boy-sobs. Breathe. Breathe! "He's crying!"

The officer knelt down. "That's you, kid. Your tears." He turned to his partner and made a half shake of his head.

Mutant–human relations—never good. Heck could hear an ambulance siren. The policeman joined his partner. Heck could hear them talking but couldn't hear what they were saying. He felt a hand on his shoulder.

"What's your name?"

"Heck. When is the ambulance going to get here? Is that his ambulance?"

"Leave him, Heck. We'll take it from here."

"Just one more—"

"We'll have to ask you to move aside."

"He's just a kid! Someone should be taking care of him."

"Hey, look who's talking."

The two policemen took Heck by the arms and pulled

him gently away while two paramedics worked on Marion. They opened his shirt and checked for a pulse. His chest was so white it was blue in the moonlight. Sorry, Heck thought. Sorrysorrysorrysorry ...

"Cervical splint?" one paramedic asked the other.

"For practice. Do a tube, too."

Heck hiccuped. "Marion ..."

One of the policemen looked suddenly interested. "Marion? Marion Ewald?"

Heck nodded. His whole body jerked with the force of a big, gut-wrenching hiccup.

"Marion Ewald. I hear this kid's been caught on just about every high place in town. His father said he was trying to jump. I guess he finally got his wish."

Heck just stood there hiccuping uncontrollably. He wanted to explain about the alien spores, but one of the officers said, "I think you better come with us and tell us exactly what happened here."

Speedlines.

Speedlines ... but there was no power in him to move.

They began packing Marion into the ambulance.

"They'll be able to help him in the hospital, right?"

"Heck, I'm sorry, but the best thing we can do for Marion is find out what happened to him. So you tell me, okay?"

Heck's teeth were knocking so hard he thought they'd shatter like cracked glass. "It was the n-night Marion had to re-release the s-spores so they could c-catch their asteroid," he said between hiccups.

The police officer said, "Uh-huh."

"That's what Marion said. That's what he was doing at the parking garage, releasing his po-pocket creatures. Can I come with him to the hospital? I'm his only fr-friend, and maybe if he hears my voice ..."

"I don't think that would be a good idea, Heck. I'm sorry."

Heck heard the ambulance worker say, "We don't need lights and sirens. He's dead."

The next hiccup wrenched his whole body.

"Hey!" the officer called to the ambulance driver. "Can you keep it down?"

Heck's whole body was shaking now. He tried to clamp down on it, hold himself still, but that just made it worse.

Dead.

As in dead.

That was a word that didn't stay in word bubbles. It was too heavy and real for cartoons, took up too much space for a two-dimensional being like himself. Heck swallowed the word. It hurt going down. He gasped with the hurt of it.

He felt like he'd jumped off fantasy land and smashed face first into reality. He was as flat as the microverse poised between eternal expansion and imminent implosion. Marion was dead, and it was his fault.

"Where do you live, Heck?" the officer asked.

"I don't know. I lost my mom." Time and space were curving, bending. "Can I call my friend, Spence? Spence Carter?"

"We'll call him for you, son. What's his number?"

Strange—Heck couldn't remember his number, and then everything went black.

Friday, May 6

It was strange to wake up from some black place where you weren't there—where you didn't exist, like you were dead.

Like Marion was dead.

Heck moaned.

Everything was clear now. Spence was right. The Good Deed was a figment of his overactive imagination. No, it was worse than that. It was an errant weapon that had killed Marion.

Someone had ripped up the fabric of space-time. He could see the whole stringy microverse before his eyes, he could see that he'd been making up his whole life so far. He was no hero. He was just a kid, a kid who was trying to save his mom from hypertime when he was in it himself.

He was so flat his heart was a collapsed star and everything was very clear. He was in the null zone, and as far as he could see, there were no events on his event horizon.

Marion was dead.

That was the one clear, clean thing in his mind. It was a hard fact that he could hold on to, that grounded him. From that fact he could construct a whole reality.

Heck's ears were filling up with tears. He could hear people talking, but he couldn't understand what they were saying. The hospital room could have been at the bottom of a swimming pool.

Heck wondered if a person could suffocate on his own snot. *Here lies Heck Superhero, asphyxiated by snot.* He imagined all the kinds of death he knew about: drowning, burning, cancer, car accident. Falling. He decided that death by snot was no worse than any other.

It felt good not to move. It felt good to just lie there. He wasn't hungry. Maybe he was dead and his spirit was just too Hi-Ho Stupid to get up off its smoky little butt and fly to heaven.

No.

His teeth hurt.

He was alive, and his teeth hurt.

His heart hurt, too. Or at least, it hurt where his heart would have been if he weren't a soulless cyborg who sent people to their early deaths.

Thanks, Marion had said. *Don't think you didn't do a good thing for me.*

Yeah, sure, a good thing. A Good Deed. He'd Good-Deeded Marion right over the railing and ...

You'll find your mom, Heck, he'd said.

"AARGH!" Heck cried aloud.

Heck's arm was attached to an IV. He pulled the tube out. Blood started dripping from the part left in his arm. He ripped the tape away and pulled the rest out. He stumbled into the bathroom and looked in the mirror.

There were black shadows under his eyes and his face was white. He'd morphed into a ghoul.

He opened a closet, found his clothes, and started dressing. They smelled bad, but he had to get out of here, go to Spence's, go to school. His legs shook as he put on his pants. His sketching pencil was in his pocket. It felt strange, like it was too small for his hand.

He stepped into the hall and looked both ways. No armed guards. There was someone in a wheelchair a little way down the hall to the right. To the left a patient was shuffling along, muttering to himself. Heck ducked back into the room to wait for the all-clear.

Heck thought about what he'd say when he got to school. "Mr. Bandras," he'd say, "sorry I'm late."

Or maybe he would say, "I saw someone die."

No. He would say, "I saw Marion Ewald die. I saw my friend die. He was just a kid."

And Mr. B., he'd probably say, "Where's your portfolio?"

Mr. Bandras had to have that portfolio. He wouldn't forget about it. He'd come looking for Heck. You didn't want to make him mad. Mr. Bandras would say, "You're late." He would say, "You're not going to believe this Mrs. B. made me peanut butter sandwiches today she knows I hate peanut butter sandwiches you'd think after twenty-nine years of marriage ..." He would say, "Where's your assignment?"

It felt good to think about Mr. B. and assignments, as if he were just some ordinary kid. Not a superhero, just an Ordinary Kid who needed help. Whose mom needed help, bigger help than she could get from her Ordinary Kid. He'd seen something in Marion when he painted him, and again in the molecular joining. He'd seen that Marion needed big help, but he'd just kept right on pretending with him, pretending he was some kind of superhero who could save Marion, when all along he was just an Ordinary Kid. Spence was right. There was no molecular joining. If there were, Heck would have been able to see what was going to happen.

In the microverse of Ordinary Kid, it was ... Friday. Friday, the Day of Portfolios Due.

A portfolio due meant you didn't have time to think about alien spores that dragged kids over walls to their deaths. Having a portfolio due meant you might be an almost normal kid in school.

Yes, he had to go now, now while the police were probably on coffee break. Soon they'd return, and find that their prisoner had escaped. He peeked out again and retreated. Someone was right outside his door.

He should stay anyway. He would stay. He wouldn't run away. He'd tell the police about his lost mom. He would go to jail, pay his debt to society, spend the rest of his days on death row ...

"Heck?" It was spoken so softly he could barely hear. But he heard.

He turned.

"Heck, honey?"

There she stood, born late and late ever since, the most beautiful mother in the world.

Heck stared.

Was he seeing things?

Was he making her up?

She just stood there in a hospital robe, staring back at him. She looked like a little girl who'd just gotten out of bed. "I've been waiting for you to wake up," she said softly.

He'd never thought of looking for her here.

He stood staring at her, so full of words he couldn't think which one to put first. At last he said, "Mom."

He put his arms around her, and she put her arms around him weakly, as if it took all her strength to do it, as if she'd forgotten how.

"Are you okay?" she whispered.

He nodded, and then he shook his head, and then he cried like a stupid little baby and not even like a boy—just a baby, waa waa. Not a superhero, not even a flat superhero, just a round little baby. He thought of Marion's thirteen-dimple smile, just before he—

"Mom."

"Sorry," she whispered. "Sorry."

The police officer came down the hall. "So I see you found each other," he said. He cleared his throat while Heck wiped his face with his sleeve. "We, uh, we haven't told your mom the details."

His mom glanced at the police officer and the nurse, then looked back at Heck.

She waited for Heck to speak, but the officer spoke first. "The boy's half starved, ma'am," he said.

"Dehydrated," the nurse said coldly.

"There was an incident with one Marion Ewald, indigent. Committed suicide. Your boy here has had a pretty traumatic time of it. We spoke to his friend, Spence Carter, who tells us Heck's been sleeping in a car for a few days."

His mom looked down. She said nothing.

Heck could see it coming. The officer felt sorry for him right now. Everyone felt sorry for him right now, poor little victim of cyclical bad parenting. But any minute now, when they saw he wasn't going to turn in his mom, they'd all walk away, throw their hands in the air.

The nurse must have gotten tired of waiting for Heck's mom to speak up. "Heck, your mom was found wandering in the early morning hours disoriented. We didn't know who she was at first."

Of course they would bring her to a hospital, Heck thought. They wouldn't know who she was. She wouldn't have been carrying a purse. A purse was too complicated an item for her. Money, bus pass, and lip gloss in her pocket were all the weight of the world she could endure.

He could see his mother's throat quiver. "I thought we made arrangements for you to stay at Spence's," she said softly. He could tell she wasn't okay. Her voice sounded sore, wounded. He noticed that her watch was three hours off.

"Yeah," Heck said. "Spence's."

Her eyes thanked him and she turned to the officer. "I

thought it was all arranged," she said.

"Yeah?" The officer jerked his chin toward Heck. "So why weren't you there?"

His eyes were already giving up. Heck looked away. He felt sorry for the cop, for his mom, for the nurse who'd had to take off his dirty socks, especially for Marion, for everyone in the whole freaking world ...

The officer said, "Excuse me," and left, and the nurse followed.

Heck's mom took her ring off and put it on the other hand. Then she changed it back to the previous hand. She did it again, and then again. Heck put his hand over hers to stop her.

"They've decided to give me some new medication," she said to her hands.

He held her hand. It was cool and dry and small.

She looked up at him, right into his eyes. They'd been molecularly joined for so long he couldn't even remember when it had happened. They didn't even have to try.

Looking in her eyes like that, he remembered that she'd never learned the difference between a.m. and p.m. Like a kid who has to translate English for his immigrant parents, he'd always had to help her with left and right, and north and south, east and west. He had to help her fill out forms and use a banking machine.

He remembered, too, all the great things about having a mom like his. She was the kind of mom who would some- times sit down with him in front of the TV at 8 a.m. and play video games with him all day. She didn't know that mornings meant cereal and supper meant macaroni. Meals were interchangeable, sleep time was negotiable, and homework time was optional. She would bake cookies for him at 3 a.m. if he had a bad dream, and never complained when he turned his music on at 5 a.m. because that was when he liked to draw and paint.

"I love you, Mom. I was worried about you," Heck said.

"You're my hero, hon."

"No."

Her hand trembled.

"I'm not a hero. I'm just a kid."

Her eyes moved around the room nervously. "Well. Well, I'm glad, at least, that everything's okay."

"I'm not okay, either, Mom."

She dropped her eyes. She couldn't stand for him not to be okay. He'd learned that so long ago he couldn't remember when he didn't know it. He had to be okay, not for his own sake, but for hers. It was a burden that she couldn't carry in any pocket for him not to be okay.

"Mom."

He held her hand the way Marion had held his, like it was a thing to be wondered at. He'd found her, just like Marion said he would. Maybe the Good Deed did change the microverse, but not always the way you thought. How could he tell her about pocket aliens leading you to worlds where you didn't exist, or how a painting that made you really look made him more of a hero than drawing a hundred superheroes? How could he explain to her that you couldn't make quantum reality without first observing it?

"We have to stop pretending that Everything's Okay. Because we need some help. Don't we, Mom?"

She shrugged.

"I know you lost your job at the Pepper Bar."

She nodded at her feet.

"We have to trust some people. We have to ask for help. Everything isn't okay, Mom, but it will be if we get some help, right?"

She looked at him, and her eyes were twelve and her mouth was sixty. Even her body couldn't stay in one time and dimension. He was breaking the trust. Tears came to her eyes, and Heck suddenly couldn't think straight.

Then he remembered the art assignment for Mr. Bandras, and he remembered he was going topworld. He wasn't going to play himself and his mom out of the microverse anymore. He was going to deal with the one they were in.

"I'll tell Mr. Bandras about my semester artwork. And the Carters about my teeth. And that we don't have a place to stay."

"No," she said.

"No?"

"No," she said. "I'll tell them. I'll go for help."

"Maybe once you're out of the hospital."

"No. I can do it. I've already started getting help, and I—I can do it."

She looked at him a long moment. "Have you been doing

your homework?" She'd never asked him that before. It felt ... good. He thought about all the work he'd missed and what he was going to have to do to catch up.

He grinned. "Well, I do have this art assignment due today."

"Okay, find something you can work on. I'm going to go talk to someone."

Heck was working on a self-portrait on hospital graph paper when Spence came into the room.

"Shhh. I snuck in," he said. He poked at the hardware behind Heck's bed. He was trying not to look Heck in the eye. "So, new Fortress of Solitude?"

Heck shrugged.

"Guess you failed in your mission to bring peace and joy to the entire planet." He fiddled with the blood pressure cuff. He put it on Heck's arm.

"I'm still young," Heck said.

Spence pumped the blood pressure cuff. "I'm sorry about your friend," he said. He sounded sad, almost as sad as Heck felt.

The cuff was getting too tight. "Hey!" He pushed Spence away and released the blood pressure cuff that was about to amputate his arm. They both laughed, and then they both stopped laughing. "Well, thanks for caring," Heck said finally.

"I guess it's the molecular joining," Spence said.

Heck stared. In a world of quantum jumps, no one could

predict where a particle would end up. Even scientists could only explain five percent of reality. The other ninety-five percent of the universe, of reality, of everything, they called dark matter. They didn't know anything about it, not even whether it was dark.

There was a soft knock at the door, and Mr. Bandras walked in.

"Hey, Mr. B.," Heck said in his best suck-up voice.

"Heck. Spence." Mr. Bandras nodded at Spence and came closer to the bed. He looked more awkward in a hospital room than in a police station.

"I'm glad you're here," Heck said in a rush, before he could chicken out. "I have to tell you—that portfolio you gave me is gone. All my work was in it."

Heck was ready for the tirade, the lecture, the inevitable F in Art. He was ready. It was all part of his new plan to interface with reality whenever necessary. Then, as soon as Mr. B. was all yelled out, he'd ask for help. What if he worked all summer at some projects, he'd ask. Could he still pass?

He wasn't prepared for what Mr. Bandras said.

"You pass, Heck. The painting makes up for all of it."

"Painting?"

"I was expecting pencil. You gave me oils."

Heck looked at Spence, who shrugged. Then he remembered. "You mean ... the Art Store?" He felt himself flushing.

"I was one of the judges at the high school art competition," Mr. B. said. His mouth was mad, but his eyes were glad.

"Did I win anything?" Heck asked.

"Of course not. You're not good enough yet. They said something, though. Do you want to hear it?"

Heck nodded.

"'This artist demonstrates an otherworldly talent.'"

Heck smiled. In a universe that was part math and part magic, maybe there was a way to integrate his kid self and his good-deed-doing self after all. He wondered if Mr. B. would let him paint him.

"Well?" Mr. Bandras said. "What have you got to say for yourself?"

Heck opened his mouth and out came "I'm hungry."

Mr. Bandras said something about thank goodness because of Mrs. B. and tomato sandwiches, and then he folded Heck in his arms, squeezing him small, small as a little kid, and Heck felt on top of the world.